This book belongs to

....

For Tessa, who is a bird
and an angel, and has my whole heart

The Calling of Jackdaw Hollow

Kate Gordon

UQP

Prologue

Jackdaw Hollow was called to this world, quick and sharp as bird claw. He burst into life faster than blinking. It was as if he felt it in his bones, this desperate need to *begin.*

In truth, it felt like a hundred years that his parents had longed for a child. Jackdaw was born under an apple-shed roof in biting frost, midwinter, as the fog rolled over the katydid-green hills of the Midlands.

And now that he was here, his parents were determined he'd make his mark on everything. They whispered the truth of it into his ear and kissed it into being.

'He's destined for greatness, this one,' his father said into his night-black hair. 'He'll take on this orchard in the palm of his hand, and he'll turn it and turn it until it's the grandest and finest—'

His wife held up her hand. 'Perhaps he is destined for greatness,' she said, 'but it will be at a thing of his very own choosing, for he is his very own boy. All we can do is love him, and love him, and watch what he becomes.'

The boy's father nodded. 'Of course,' he whispered. 'Of course.' And he pulled her close, his beautiful Thelma, and they cradled their son inside their arms, and nothing could be more perfect than that. Nothing could be so *alive.*

Thelma Hollow named her boy 'Jackdaw', after a bird she saw peeping in the nursery window on the morning he arrived into the world. The bird looked as if it were searching for something shiny and new. Thelma saw that self-same look in her small boy's black-button eyes. He was searching, searching, even then, for the thing that would make him shine.

For his first few months, Jackdaw's life was milk and apple sauce, and so many kind-eyed strangers coming to call and check on his growth. He was doted on by his parents and by the folk of the Midlands. And yet he never seemed content with it. He wailed and wailed, and his parents despaired. But, oh, they loved him. How they loved him, to the furthest reaches of the stars.

But *then* ...

But then the lightning came.

It was a year later, midwinter again, and stormy with it – winters in the Midlands were only ever blue and crystal-sparkling or thunder-cloud furious. This night, the heavens threw their ire down as if the island itself were the source of all things vexing in the world.

Jack Hollow didn't know, yet, what was meant by thunder, what a calamity could be brought by the lighting-up of pitch-dark sky.

He lay in his small wooden cot, restless and squalling. The storm was over yonder still, away and past the hills. But it was sniffing around, closer, closer. It would soon find the scent of that cosy orchard house.

His parents, at the end of their wits and sleepless from so many nights of Jackdaw crying, had a notion to provide their boy with a diversion. Something to stop the wailing, just for a little while. Something bright and shiny.

Something like a lightning bolt.

Thelma called out to the girl in the kitchen, 'Put the kettle on, so we can have hot tea when we get inside, and then go home now, won't you? This storm will surely grow wilder. Get home and safe and warm.'

The small family left the safety of their cosy house and walked apace, the parents glancing at times at the sky. The mother held Jackdaw tight in her arms – her tiny, howling heart in a boy.

They trusted the apple trees to protect them. After all, the trees had always looked after them, given them their livelihood and their wealth, and the love and respect of the Midlands people.

They stood beneath the sturdiest tree to watch the lightning, faraway.

And Jackdaw was silent. Jackdaw was *happy* in the arms of his mother, watching the shining, shining sky.

They didn't expect the lightning would come so close, so fast.

But that is the way of death, isn't it?

It is always close. It is always fast. It is always, ever, shining.

Jackdaw Hollow's parents were struck. Perhaps he was struck, too, but only a little – his mother's love protecting him from the worst of it. In any case, they left this world, when the bolt hit, but Jackdaw Hollow stayed.

Jackdaw Hollow was found in the still-teeming rain, whimpering and full of dismay, by the groundsman of a grand house nearby, who was searching for a lost bird. The bird had belonged to his son. His boy no longer lived, but the bird did, and the man could not bear the thought of losing it, too.

The man who found Jackdaw Hollow had a face like the side of a rocky hill, lines on his cheeks like dolerite columns. He had two furry eyebrows and a nose like a cliff. His eyes were unmistakeably kind.

He heard the kettle, screeching and wailing. To his one good ear it sounded a bit like birdsong.

'What's this?' Walter Hardbread said to his dog.

And then he saw Henry and Thelma. He shook his head at all the sadness of the world and he scooped Jackdaw up into his rasp-skinned arms and, carrying the baby, now silent, he embarked on two errands.

The first was to the town's police officer to tell him about Thelma and Henry.

The second was to Mrs Celeste Beekman, the headmistress at Direleafe Hall.

★

Mrs Beekman sat by her window, in the cottage beside Direleafe Hall, listening to the storm. The knock on the door made her jump, and the news the old man delivered felt like a knife in her belly.

'Not the Hollows!' Mrs Beekman moaned, a hand pressed to her mouth. She beckoned Mr Hardbread inside, shaking her head at the injustice of all of it. 'How is it possible for such a horror to be visited upon such good people? Such good friends? And a *baby* ...'

Mr Hardbread nodded. 'A baby. Which is why, Celeste, I've come to you.'

Mrs Beekman looked confused and then her eyebrows rose. She shook her head. 'Mr Hardbread, Direleafe is a school for *girls*.'

'You don't 'ave to take him on as a pupil, like,' Mr Hardbread said, proffering the child to Mrs Beekman like a gifted loaf of bread.

Mrs Beekman looked down at him. The boy had cool brown skin and hair like dark, tufty feathers. And there was a strangeness about his eyes. They were gleaming, marble-like, *metal-like*, as if they had been forged in fire. *Or lightning*, Mrs Beekman supposed.

'Some sort of servant boy, perhaps?' Mr Hardbread suggested.

'He is a baby,' Mrs Beekman cried. 'What good is a servant *baby*? He can barely stand by himself, let alone reach the mantelpieces to dust them!'

'Well, not now, o' course!' the groundsman replied, smiling despite all the misery of the day. 'But some time or t'other, soon, when he's grown a bit.'

'And until then? I'm supposed to raise him? Feed him milk and pumpkin? Give him wooden blocks and toys on wheels? That's not my job, sir. I am a schoolmistress, not a nanny! He has family, surely! Aunts or uncles, or—'

But Mr Hardbread shook his head. For everyone knew, of course, that Henry and

Thelma had been the last of the Hollow family. A plague from across the world had picked the rest off, one by one, just as it had done to so many of the girls of Direleafe Hall. It was part of what made the couple so precious.

'No family? Right, so. Then what about you and your wife?'

Mr Hardbread sighed, gazing down at his beaten leather boots. 'We had a boy,' he said, quietly. 'The wife never wanted another, when he went ter heaven. Said she couldn't bear the pain of it. Being honest, I don't think I could, neither. It's a kind of mad peril, ain't it, loving a child? I'm too weary and broken to risk all that again.'

Mrs Beekman stared at the old man, long and hard. She stared at the weather-lines in his brown-apple face and the aching in his eyes.

She thought of her own pain. She thought of the child she had loved and lost (it was the plague that took her, also). She sighed and she said, 'Well, all right.' And then, as

Mr Hardbread nodded – more gratitude in that nod than a thousand bellowed *thank yous* – she added, 'But not as a servant. This boy has already suffered enough. He'll be a pupil.'

'A pupil,' said Mr Hardbread, softly. 'Right enough. I would've liked to have been a pupil here. Learn to read and whatnot. But it was only for girls, of course. And the boys' school was much too far yonder ...'

Mrs Beekman nodded. 'The only boy pupil in the history of Direleafe Hall. And he will be more than that, besides. In fact, he'll be my son.'

Mrs Beekman looked over at the wood-framed mantel mirror. She looked at herself, cradling this child and, somehow, she was brought back to a time when her golden curls were not shot through with grey. To a time when she had been held by her husband, Fred, at the centenary dance. Before he went to Africa. Before he never returned.

That was the last time Mrs Beekman had felt like this. Soft inside, and hopeful.

Mrs Beekman had, the day the news about Fred arrived, hardened into the stone of a peach and she had never softened again. But now. But *now* ...

Now, Mrs Beekman had a boy.

And he was to be her son.

Mrs Beekman looked down at this baby – at *her* new baby boy – and, finally, after all those years, she felt the stone inside her crack and the almond within it was sweet. She felt joy returning to her soul. It might be a mad peril, sure enough, but loving this boy might be the making of her.

'This boy,' Mrs Beekman said, cradling him in her arms, 'survived that bolt for a reason. He was saved, to be right here.'

1
The boy

Jackdaw Hollow didn't mind it – being the only boy in a school for girls. He didn't mind it because there were worse things – he read about them in books.

War and loss and heartbreak.

He had none of those. In fact, his life was quiet and still, with each day more or less exactly like the one that came before. Each day unexceptional – as unexceptional as Jackdaw believed his own small, twelve-year-old self to be.

In fact, the very worst thing about Jackdaw Hollow's life was that he was lonely. He had

Mrs Beekman, of course, and he loved her fiercely. But he had no friends to speak of. No *proper* friends, anyhow. Not like the ones in books – whose hearts matched perfectly, entirely.

The girls at the school were pleasant and kind and clever enough, and he respected them greatly. But they weren't like him in a way that seemed much deeper than the fact that he was a boy and they were girls. No, it was more than that. It had something to do with lightning, perhaps, or something to do with souls.

The closest he had to a friend like the ones in books was Angharad, the school's apprentice cook, who tried so hard to teach him to bake pies. And it was because of Angharad – of coming to find her – that Jackdaw Hollow learned the thing that was to change his life.

Jackdaw Hollow knew, of course, that Mrs Beekman was not his mother *truly*. His birth parents were Henry and Thelma Hollow and they had perished because of a bolt from the sky and an apple tree that should have been shelter but was not.

But he never knew the *whys* and *wherefores* until this day, as he stood in the shadows, outside the kitchen, listening to the whispers.

'They say that baby never stopped crying,' a scullery girl declared. 'They say his parents took him out of doors to show him the lights in the sky. My sister worked in the orchard, you know. She put the kettle on and left and the next she heard of any of it was that the Hollow family died. And it's his fault. The baby. His wailing is what did it. It's his fault that they died.'

'It never is.' This was Angharad. 'He was a baby. How can a baby, brand new and pure, ever be blamed for *anything*? A baby ain't done nothing yet. A baby has no dreams nor calling. A baby is blank, not good nor bad. He can't have killed his parents. He couldn't have saved them, neither.'

'Well, he's got mad luck is all I can say,' the scullery girl replied. 'To live when he shouldn't have. Better hope he does something mighty grand with this life, don't you think? To make it all worthwhile.'

Jackdaw did not hear Angharad's reply. He blinked at stinging tears. He tried to blink away all he had heard, but the words were grass seeds. They clung on to his soul.

A baby has no dreams nor calling ...

It's his fault that they died ...

He pressed his back against the wall, pressed himself into the darkness. He could hear his heart, feel it, beating so strongly his body vibrated with it. He could feel his *aliveness* so much it made him shudder.

He was alive.

They were dead.

It was his fault.

He felt, suddenly, lonelier than ever.

Jackdaw didn't mind it, this being at Direleafe Hall, but he never felt quite *within* it, properly. He felt on the outside of everything. The only boy in a school for girls. An orphaned boy. A strange, prickly boy, a thistle amongst all the flowers.

And now, look, a boy who lived, erroneously. A boy who made his parents die. Or at least did not save them. A boy who *lived* but didn't, really.

Better hope he does something mighty grand with this life, don't you think? To make it all worthwhile ...

What was he doing? Nothing at all, save watching birds and the stars. Nothing at all, save climbing trees and fading into the shadows. Nothing at all, nothing at *all* to make up for having lived.

He had to fix it, somehow. This one life he'd been given – he had to make it *grand.*

But how?

2
The calling

That night, when the moon was full and the whole world seemed varnished in a kind of glimmer, magical and profound, Jackdaw Hollow lay in bed, drinking hot cocoa, Mrs Beekman on a wicker chair by his side. She had just read Jack a story about a girl called Solace, who went on a quest to find a thylacine she had seen in the woods.

'It is my calling,' Solace said, 'to find the tiger in the dark.'

Jackdaw, who found the people in books much easier to understand than people who lived outside of them, felt a candle ignite within him. '*It is my calling …*' he mouthed to himself.

'What was that?' asked Mrs Beekman.

'My calling,' Jack murmured, his eyes shining.

A baby has no dreams nor calling. A baby is blank, not good nor bad.

But it seemed to Jack that he had done bad. He had killed his parents. That was a weight in the negative of things. And a weight in the positive was a *calling.*

Solace wished to find the tiger to give her life true meaning.

What meaning did his life have?

The only boy in a school for girls. Always looking in. His parents had died and he was barely … he was barely *living.* Not like the journeying, questing heroes in his books lived. Not like Solace lived – hunting thylacines.

His parents had died – that was a weight – and he did nothing to balance it.

'I don't have a calling,' Jack said. 'Not at all.'

'That's not true,' Mrs Beekman replied. 'You like ...'

'Most things,' Jackdaw sighed. 'I like most things quite a lot, but nothing *particularly.* A calling is not liking most things. There's nothing even, really, that I completely detest.'

'Aside from mathematics,' Mrs Beekman said wryly.

Jack almost smiled. 'Well, yes,' he said. 'But even that I can endure. At least detesting would be something. It would be a strong feeling. I have no strong feelings at all. No passions ... No *callings.* I see the girls at Direleafe. Each of them seems to have their place, don't they? Some of them are good at games, with sticks and balls. Or they have a gift for music, or painting, or song.

'I have no calling, Mama. I love to read and ... I like birds and trees and the stars, but that's only watching. I don't make a bird fly or a star burn brightly. I don't burn brightly at all. I like science and climbing and learning things. What else? I would quite like to be good at baking ...'

Mrs Beekman shuddered, thinking of the last, burned offering Jackdaw had brought her. It might have been a pie.

'Angharad says she'll teach me,' Jackdaw said, defensively. 'Perhaps that will be it. My calling.'

'A calling is not something to strive over, not something to vex yourself about,' Mrs Beekman said gently. 'It is just something that settles upon you, when the time is right. It's like love, that way. It comes to you, when you're not searching for it.'

'I'll find it,' Jackdaw said firmly. 'Like Solace and the tiger. I've spent twelve years now, watching and reading and staying still. Staying ...' he remembered the word Angharad had used, 'staying *blank*. I will find my calling. I have to.'

He rolled onto his side and yawned. 'I have to,' he said, more quietly. 'I have to be special, somehow, to make up for everything.'

As his breathing slowed, Mrs Beekman put her hand on his shoulder. 'Oh, my dear boy,' she whispered. 'Don't you know? You're everything to me.'

3
The ghost girls

Jackdaw Hollow sat upon the roof of Direleafe Hall. Below him, the girls skipped and chased and played, or yawned into their opened books as they strolled about the grounds. They laughed and twirled and burst their seams with all the stuff of living.

Jackdaw watched them, for a time. He always watched them. That's what people *outside* do. They watch. And they wonder. And they imagine.

That girl there, with the rust-red curls ... Her name was Penelope and she loved to paint. He imagined her, one day, living in a big city on the other side of the world, famous and dressed in silks.

That one was Mary-Anna. She was the best in the school at tennis. He saw her, in the future, disguised as a man, muscles made big with milk and eggs, and winning every trophy.

He imagined them as characters from books. It was easier to see them that way.

He tried imagining himself. He imagined the way he looked, in the mirror of the cottage bathroom.

He saw a boy with black hair like feathers and a pointed nose and hollows beneath his cheekbones. He saw a boy who was strange-looking, his features indistinct as if he were already a memory. He saw a boy who looked like a baby bird. A boy who looked like a jackdaw.

He did not see himself painting, or holding any trophies. He was a boy who was as *blank* as a painter's canvas – a boy without a calling.

Jackdaw looked up.

Above him, birds circled. He saw starlings and blackbirds and wrens and one currawong who looked a bit like him.

He pulled out his ornithology notebook. He wrote about feathers and he wrote about beaks and he was, for a time, content. No thoughts of lightning bolts and apple trees. No thoughts of absent *callings.*

But then the clouds turned dark overhead and all the birds flew away.

And Jackdaw was melancholy again. 'I wish watching birds was a calling,' he said. 'But it's nothing like it at all.'

'What does he mean? A *calling*?'

Jackdaw Hollow didn't hear her – this speaker at his side. He did not hear her and he did not see her. He did not see *any* of them.

Despite the way it might have looked to any of the Direleafe girls strolling about the grounds – despite the way it looked to Jack Hollow himself – this gazing at birds was not done in solitude. Jack Hollow did not sit alone.

Beside him on the roof, ducks all in a row, were three unearthly girls.

Florence, Lucy and Nell.

Florence had eyes like a summer storm and hair as white as clouds. Lucy was dark-skinned and corkscrew-curled, and Nell was as small as a mouse.

Jack couldn't see the girls. Not yet.

The girl who had spoken – this one was Nell – waved a hand in front of Jackdaw's face. She sighed. 'I'm telling you. He'd see us. If you'd only let me do it.'

'Flimsy science,' Florence insisted. She crossed her arms. 'What logical reason is there, at all, for us to show ourselves?'

Lucy, the one with the biggest heart, said, 'He's sad enough, can't you see? We would be ... a reminder. Of death's closeness and everything he has lost.'

'And after all,' said Florence, 'he's had enough strangeness in his life without adding three ghosts to the mix.'

'We're not strange,' said Nell, pouting. 'We are ... exceptional. Now—' She raised an eyebrow. 'What does he mean? About *callings*?'

'It means a vocation,' said Florence airily, 'or a pursuit, like I have for science and Lucy has for kindness and you have for ...'

The two girls looked at Nell.

'I have vocations,' she told the others, her brow drawing to a scowl. 'I have *pursuits*.'

'Name one,' said Florence archly.

Nell grinned and it was wide and wicked. She pointed at the boy. 'My next pursuit,' she said, grandly, 'will be finding *him* a calling. And you two are going to help me.'

'Whatever for?' said Florence, exasperated.

'I think,' said Lucy shyly, 'that what he really needs is a friend. He looks so sad and lonely. A friend is better than a calling.'

Nell was silent, for a time, tapping on her chin. 'What if ...' she said, finally, 'we could find him both?'

And then, leaning closer, she added, 'It can't

be any of the Direleafe girls. They're nothing at all like him. But can't you think of another girl? Can't you think of the girl we see, with a bruise on her jaw and holes in her shoes and *longing* in her soul for *more* ...'

Lucy and Florence nodded. Of course, they knew this girl.

'She is *like him*,' Nell whispered. 'Odd, like him. And she is always out in the fields, seeking her own calling. Perhaps they can find their callings *together*. Two birds with one stone.'

And before either of the other ghost girls could even begin to argue, Nell took her two friends by their hands.

'Come, now,' she said. 'To the library. It's time to do some planning.'

Florence rolled her eyes. And Lucy shivered and gulped. But they went with Nell, because they always did.

4
The girl in the tulips

Jack never knew the ghost girls were there but, somehow, when they were gone, he felt their absence like a duffel coat removed.

He shivered.

He looked above again, to the darkening clouds. One by one, silver raindrops began to fall, as if the heart of the sky were breaking.

The Direleafe girls hadn't noticed, yet. They laughed and they skipped, and some read beneath trees (he liked those girls the best).

A small ache began inside him. He wished he could be like those girls. He wished they were like him. He wished he could fit, somewhere, with someone ...

No.

He shook his head. He wasn't searching for a place to fit, or a person to fit *with.* He was searching for his calling.

Angharad, the apprentice cook, walked past the girls, smiling and waving and sometimes skipping, too, when the mood took her. She was four years older than Jackdaw. Sometimes it seemed as if she were a grown-up when she taught him in the kitchen. At other times, her long plaits swinging as she skipped, she seemed like a little girl.

Jackdaw smiled at Angharad, though she could not see him doing it. He liked spending time in the kitchen with Angharad, even though he burned all the pies. Baking pies was definitely not his calling.

Jack looked past the Direleafe grounds. He looked past the high sandstone walls that surrounded the hall, past this place that was his home and not, past the gates whose fingers stretched up and up, as if they wished to grab those clouds and pull them down to Earth ...

He looked *out*, to the fields and beyond, extending his vision more and more, in the hope that he might see it – his family orchard, the homestead and that tree where one of his lives had ended and another had begun, separated by a lightning bolt.

He couldn't see it, not quite. Hills like stout pistachio cakes blocked his view. He let his eyes drift, over fields speckled with sheep and an oil-painting paddock of tulips.

And there, in the middle of the tulips, he spied a wandering form.

He thought, at first, that it might have been a bird – a white bird of prey or perhaps a seabird. After all, the form was *coloured* like a seabird – sort of off-white with greyish touches.

But then he realised the form had no wings – at least none that he could see. And it was much too tall to be a bird. And there was darkness wafting behind it, like a capelet, like hair. Long hair, and not in pigtails but *free*.

Jack had never seen a girl with hair that was free. Even Angharad's hair was secured at its ends.

And he'd never seen a girl in a dress like that. The girls at Direleafe wore dark pleated skirts that reached their mid-calves, and ruffled shirts with bows at the neck, and woollen jumpers in the wintertime.

This girl wore a loose frock, secured at the waist, with a rope, perhaps. She looked (now he could see she was *not-bird*) like those pictures in the books about Ancient Greece. She looked, it had to be said, something like an angel, with wings *invisible*. She looked like something from a dream.

She looked ...

Different.

Strange.

Peculiar.

He had never seen a girl like her before.

He watched her running through the tulips, her head tilted back to drink in the sun. All of a sudden, the girl seemed to *flip*, like windmill sails turning.

She disappeared into the tulips, as if she had never existed, and Jackdaw found himself staring at the space she had left, wondering if he had imagined her.

5
The proposition

At night-time, the ghost girls came to Jackdaw.

He woke with a start when the clock hand moved to midnight and sat up straight as a pin feather in his cosy, warm nest of a bed. Below his attic bedroom, the house was creaking and sighing, settling into the night. He could hear Mrs Beekman moving about, perhaps to get a glass of water.

It wasn't his mother who had woken him.

They stood at the end of his bed – three girls, painted with moonlight and staring and smiling.

He wasn't afraid. He'd read enough books to imagine anything possible and to know that ghosts were not always bad, just as humans were not always good.

He somehow felt as if he knew these girls, as if he had been waiting, always, for them to appear.

'Hello, Jackdaw.'

The ghost girl looked, to Jack, like an ermine – skinny as a noodle, all mouth and ears.

And her eyes – her eyes saw right through him. They were small scalpels, cutting and *scooping* out everything he was.

He swallowed, hard.

He closed his eyes.

Maybe the ghosts will disappear.

He opened his eyes.

They did not.

He looked at the other two. One of them had science in her eyes. He recognised that. She looked like she might enjoy birdwatching, too.

The other was a will-o'-the-wisp, a puff of smoke and sweetness. She looked as if she might be good at holding, good at giving comfort. Just like Mrs Beekman was.

The first of them spoke again. 'I'm Nell,' she said. 'This is Florence and Lucy. We are ...'

'*Ghosts*,' Jack whispered.

She nodded. 'Of course. Though we are quite new to that side of things. We were alive not so very long ago. I died first.' She said this with pride, as if she had won a running race.

'Jack ... Jackdaw Hollow,' he replied, his voice trembling ever so slightly. He blinked. 'How is this possible? How are you possible?'

'You have an imagination, don't you?' asked Lucy, shyly. 'Ghosts are only the perfect meeting point of science and imagination.' She smiled, pink-cheeked. 'Like you.'

Jackdaw tried to cling to that word – *perfect.* But it slipped away, no matter how hard he tried. He was not perfect. He was the furthest thing from it. He was a skinny, friendless boy who had no calling.

His birth parents were perfect – loved and generous and *vibrant.* They were glowing crystalline stones, pressed into shining smoothness and held close by those who adored and admired them.

'You,' Florence added, as if she saw something in his eyes, 'are a thing not possible – a boy who should not have survived.'

That was true. Jack was impossible. Impossible and broken and shouldn't-be.

Unless ...

Until ...

Until he found his calling. Then, he would glow.

Florence continued, 'A boy who should be *one of us*. But you are here and not-dead – impossibly – so how is it that you can't believe in us?'

'I do believe in you,' Jack answered, boldly. 'I just don't understand the science of it.'

'The science is simple,' said Florence. 'I'm learning it, you see. Some bits are flimsy and some are solid. This is solid. Human beings are nine parts body and one part soul and the dying only takes the body part.'

'But you still have ... bodies,' Jack pointed out. 'I can *see* your bodies.'

'They're not bodies. Not really. Only the memory of bodies,' Florence replied, matter-of-factly, as if it were nothing.

'We're all just memories,' said Lucy, in a whisper. 'Memories and stories, written on the walls of this place. Direleafe Hall holds us together.'

'It holds me together, too,' said Jack.

'But it's not enough,' Nell replied, eyes glinting. 'It's not enough to be held together. Sometimes you need to burst from your skin. You need to find—'

'A calling.'

'Precisely. That's why we are here.'

Jack's brow furrowed. 'You are here to give me a calling?' He shook his head. 'My mother says that one will find me. I thought that I should find it myself ...'

Nell shook her head. 'But look-it! Instead, we have found you one. We have found you *her*.'

Her.

Jack thought of the girl in the tulip field. He thought of the way she tumbled ...

Could it be ...?

'You saw her,' whispered Lucy. 'I can see it in your eyes.'

Jack sucked in a breath.

Could it ...?

'A girl can't be it,' Jack protested, weakly. 'A girl can't be a calling.'

'He's right, you know,' said Florence, folding her arms. 'This is a terrible idea.'

'I thought perhaps painting,' Jack said, 'for my calling ...'

'A girl might not be a calling,' said Nell, 'but *saving* a person could be.'

6
No better time than now

'We never talked about saving,' said Florence.

Jack's head jerked up. 'Saving from what?'

A lightning bolt.

A storm.

A baby is blank, not good nor bad. He can't have killed his parents. He couldn't have saved them, neither.

'She won't want it,' Florence insisted. 'She's not the sort of girl who will want saving.'

Nell ignored her. 'Jackdaw Hollow, when life presents you with an opportunity like this, you take it.' Her voice quietened. 'When life presents you with *anything*, you take it.'

'Saving from what?' Jack asked again.

Lucy walked to the window. The moonlight seemed to shine through her. It made her silver. It made her magic. 'I thought this would be about kindness,' she said.

'I think this is about *Nell*,' Florence replied.

Jack folded his arms. 'I still don't understand. Why are you here, really? What do any of you care about me, or my calling? What of anything have I or ... or this *girl* got to do with the three of you?'

Nell clasped her hands. 'Can I tell you a story?' she asked.

Jack nodded. He might be befuddled and a little disquieted, but a story told by a ghost seemed like the sort of thing a person should never refuse.

'I was a student at Direleafe Hall,' Nell said. 'I fell from a cherry tree, on my twelfth birthday – unfortunate but then, I was attempting to steal cherries ... for, well, never you mind the why.' She shot a terse look at Lucy, when she said this, and Lucy, blazing-cheeked, bit her lip and looked away.

'The stealing is the thing and, furthermore, stealing cherries *was* expressly forbidden at Direleafe Hall. So, I suppose I had something coming to me, but I do consider death was a touch severe. Anyhow, my point is, death wasn't so bad, really. A bit frightening and bewildering but so was life. The only real difference with death is nobody sees you ...'

'Nobody sees me anyway,' said Jack. 'Aside from my mother.'

'One person is enough,' Lucy whispered out the window, out to the moon.

Nell didn't hear her or perhaps she pretended. 'But life ... I didn't realise it at the time, but life was better. Life is the *thing*, Jackdaw Hollow. And you're not living it.'

Jack lifted his chin. 'I will be. When I find my calling.'

Nell smiled, triumphantly. 'And so, we present, your calling!' She gave a bow.

'But—' Florence began.

Nell shot her a look that could melt bones.

'A person isn't a calling,' Jack said again, feebly. But he was thinking of his parents and how he had made them die. He thought of what Angharad had said, too. He had been too small, too *weak*, to save them.

But this girl ...

No.

A person wasn't a calling.

Nell sighed. 'All right, then,' she said. 'If not that ... at least get to know her some. This girl Angeline is magnificent at following her calling. She could teach you a trick or two.'

'I could do that,' said Jack. 'That's better.'

Nell raised a shoulder. 'And you might find, when you get to know her, that the *saving* thing just ... happens.'

'Nell!' Florence cried.

Nell only growled in reply.

'You still haven't told me why,' said Jack. 'Why me? Why you? Why *her*?'

‘I see you, Jackdaw Hollow,’ said Nell, quietly. She peered at Jack. And Jack felt, for a moment, as if he were the ghost. As if she could see all that he was, inside and out. As if she could see the soul of him.

The hollow in his soul.

‘If someone had seen me,’ Nell went on, ‘running to that cherry tree and bade me stop, I would be thankful for it. I did one wild thing before I died – perhaps I even did two, if you count the cherry tree – and I’m grateful for it. But I wish I did more. I see you, Jackdaw Hollow. I see you *not living.* I am telling you: live more wildly, more fully. Now.’

There was a long pause. The girls stood at the foot of his bed, staring at Jack, and Jack felt a heat creep up from his toes to the tips of his ears. He knew he should say more, but he didn’t know what and, finally, Nell stomped. ‘Well?’ she exclaimed. ‘Are you waiting for a lion to run in and bite you on the ankles?’

Jack's brow furrowed. 'I don't know what you—'

'Go to her! Go and find her!'

'Now?'

Nell rolled her eyes. 'Jack Hollow,' she said, 'didn't you hear me? I died when I was twelve years old. Therefore I do know this one simple fact: there is no better time than *now*.'

Jack stared at this tiny, terrifying ghost girl. 'All right,' he said, because any other response seemed impossible. 'I'll go.'

Nell nodded, triumphantly. 'You'll see,' she said. 'You'll see – it will work. You'll see and then you'll thank me.' She shimmered then, and she faded.

Lucy faded, too.

Only Florence remained. 'Please listen to me,' she said. 'Angeline doesn't need saving. She wants to save herself.'

'I won't,' said Jackdaw. 'I'll only watch her. I'll watch her and learn and then I will find my calling.'

'And be her friend, perhaps?' added Florence.

Jack's nose wrinkled. 'I'm not good at that.'

Florence raised her eyebrows. 'Scientists never tell themselves a thing cannot be done. They only ever tell themselves that they will *try*.'

Jack took that in and turned it round like a stone inside his head. 'I'll try,' he told Florence.

She disappeared then, too, and Jack was all alone.

'Wait!' he called out after her. 'I don't know how to do this. I don't know how to have a friend. *I don't know how ...*' He whispered the last part. But even as he said it, he stood and made for the door. He knew, somehow, that not knowing shouldn't prevent a person from trying.

After all, he could stay here, now, entangled in all of it. Or he could step outside, into the night, and find the girl who might help him to step outside of all of it.

7
First meeting

The girl in the tulip field turned, heels over head, like foam-topped waves rolling to shore. Above her, the moonlight made the shape of her, the paleness of her, more stark, more visible. She seemed at odds with the landscape. A thing outside, separate. *Above* it all.

She turned three times, and then four, and then fell to the dirt with a curse word that made Jack Hollow blush. He saw her hole-toed boots sticking out from above the tops of the tulips.

He heard her cursing again as the boots disappeared and her head – hair wild as brambles and, now, decorated with red and yellow petals – appeared. The expression on her face was thunderous.

She shook her head, once, twice, and then she faced Jack Hollow. The thunderclouds grew – darker, wilder. She stood so her whole body was visible above the tops of the flowers. Up close, her white dress was streaked with mud and flower pollen.

Jackdaw smiled at her – as big as he could, as big as he'd ever smiled before. Even though she looked slightly alarming, smiling was all he could think of to do.

He hoped he didn't look peculiar. But how are you supposed to smile at a girl who you're meeting for the first time in a tulip field, at the suggestion of a ghost? And what do you say – to a girl, to anyone – to make them be your friend?

He took a deep breath, and he said to her, through the smile, through his too-big teeth, 'My name is Jackdaw Hollow, and I am here to invite you ... to beseech you ... to, to ... *instruct you ...*'

He cleared his throat. *Instruct* ... Instruct was not right, not a bit. And neither was 'command' or 'direct', or any of the other synonyms he could think of to simply say, *'You must like me!'*

And he shouldn't say anything about ghosts and nothing at all about callings. Not yet. She almost certainly would find all of that peculiar.

'I am here,' he tried again, 'to *make* you my *friend*!'

Before he had begun his talking, her face might have been alarming, but it was also, in a way, *open* – a tulip with its petals unfurled.

And now?

Now, her petals had closed.

Now, her arms were crossed over her woollen shawl. Her tattered, hobnail boot *tap, tap, tapped* on the broken stones and withered flower bulbs beneath her feet. Now, in the place of her wide-lipped mouth, there was a line so hard and so straight it seemed quill-inked on her skin.

Her eyebrows were dark millipedes, arching on her dirt-stained face, as if in a question or some form of contempt.

She made his heart shrivel breakfast-fig small. When he had first spotted her, his heart had been as big as the moon.

'Jackdaw Hollow?' she said, her tone all accusation, as if *Jackdaw Hollow* was a truly disgraceful thing to be.

'Yes!' he blurted. 'Jack, really. And ...' he was desperate, now, 'I am ... well, I don't suppose you know this about me but ... when I was a baby, I survived a lightning bolt, which means I'm a kind of miracle ... I mean ...' He felt his cheeks burning. 'I mean, *it* was a miracle, but I suppose I am a bit special, too, to have survived that. I mean ... I mean to say ...' His voice trailed away like cigar smoke.

He didn't know, even a bit, why he said any of it, except to – perhaps – make those eyebrows flatten or that ink-line mouth curve upwards, but as soon as the words came out, he regretted them. He regretted them so much that he clamped his hand across his lips, as if trying to shove the words back in.

But the worst thing was that the line did not curve, and the eyebrows did not flatten, and those crossed arms did not fall by her sides.

She did not like him, one bit, and maybe even *less* for his odd and big-headed proclamation.

She would never be his friend.

She would never help him find his calling.

All was lost, again.

He was lost, again.

'Special? Is that so? Are you *special*, Jack Hollow?' she asked, and an eyebrow arched even more. 'And what makes you sure of that?'

'I didn't mean it,' he mumbled. 'The special part. I'm not special at all, really, though some people say I am on account of me surviving a lightning bolt. But it was my fault I was out there in the first place. It was all a cosmic mistake, unless—'

Unless I can find my calling. And I need you to help me ...

But he couldn't say that, of course.

All was lost, again.

He was lost, again.

Her brow furrowed. 'Well, I don't know what a *cosmic mistake* is, but I have heard about this lightning bolt. I heard about your parents. Thelma and Henry, am I right? Yes, I've heard everything about them, from Mr Hardbread. Real pillars of the community, I believe. And you their only son, *survived.*

'But didn't you know? We're not so very unalike. My parents died as well, you see, not by a lightning bolt, but because they were poor and poor people die all the time and nobody cares or says their children are *special.* Nobody even bats an eyelid because it is just the way of things. So, my parents died, in agony, and I watched and I cried and I wished with all my heart that they would not die and I prayed to every God that they would not die, but they *did* die, despite it all, because *that is the way of things* and when they didn't breathe any more, I ran into the streets, screaming and wailing, and not one person scooped me into their arms and said, "*This girl is special and a miracle.*"

'Instead, they smacked my buttocks and they hushed me and sent me off to a grand house overseen by a mean woman and I – all of five tender, fearful years – was set to work, scrubbing and being beaten soundly if I did not scrub hard enough or had the wrong expression on my face. And I have scrubbed ever since. And I have *survived.* I think many other girls mightn't have.

'But I did, for I am fierce and I know that my calling is elsewhere and other than this time right now. I *survived* for I was meant to survive. But nobody ever congratulated me. And never once, in those seven years hence, have I *ever* been called special. My only friends are rabbits and birds and mice and now, it seems, *you* – the most *special and magnificent*

Jack Hollow. Aren't I *lucky and favoured*, now?'

Angeline finally took a breath. When she exhaled, it shone shivery against the darkness like the puff of an angry dragon.

Jack understood. Much as his heart ached for the crushed-stone way she spoke, he understood her anger. Here was he – Jack Hollow – in his fine clothes, with his educated accent and his knowledge of literature and Latin and ornithology and, yes, even mathematics, and she stood before him in that shawl that was more hole than wool, and he came to her full of such ready ownership and then declared himself *special* when she did not bow before him immediately?

Of course, she did not like him.

Of course, she would never be his friend.

Here was he, with the privilege of a happy childhood and a comfortable bed and the love of a mother, adopted though she may be, and then declaring himself *not special, not lucky, not favoured* ...

He was lost.

'I'm sorry,' he whispered, a pressure in his throat like so many tears, rising, mutinying. He turned because he did not wish to see her face when the tears began their charge.

It seemed so ineffectual, his apology. No more useful than a stone placed on a beach in the face of a tsunami.

He was no more useful than a stone.

How can a stone be a friend to a girl like this, wild and wicked and clever and tumbling?

How can a stone have any kind of calling?

But then ...

'Wait!'

Jack stopped, his toe scuffing into the dust beneath the rocks, sending a plume of it upwards. He did not turn. His face was still glazed with tears and he knew they would shine in the moonlight.

He heard crunching on the stones behind him. He used the sleeve of his shirt to wipe at his face, but he knew his cheeks would still be pink. He was afraid to turn because of the pinkness and also – what if she had a mind to sock him in the jaw, for all his arrogance?

But then there was a hand landing on his shoulder, soft, as if a bird had settled there.

He could feel her breath on his neck.

She said, 'Jack Hollow, I might need to pluck some of that *snobbishness* out from under that skin of yours, but you're an acceptable human, I think. You'll not beseech me or command me or *make* me. *I* will choose. I will choose you to be my friend. Not because I need you. I don't need anyone but myself. But I've been practising my circus tricks for such a long time on my own. It might be useful to have an audience.'

When Jack looked at her, confused, she rolled her enormous eyes. 'I'm going to join the circus one day, Jack Hollow. I practise skills I might use, out in the tulip field. When the time is right, I'm going to run away across the Midlands Moors and I will join a troupe.

And they will be my family and my friends and, well, I'm afraid I've had neither of those since my parents died. I've had nobody to watch me. What use is a performer without an audience?' She smiled. 'So, that's my condition.'

'Oh, yes! I will. Of course, I'll be your—'

Angeline shook her head, silencing him. 'I have more, still.' She held up three grubby fingers, the nails cracked and caked in dirt. She folded down her ring finger. 'You don't ever try to command me again.'

Jack nodded.

She held down her middle finger. 'You don't *ever* ask me to do any duties for you. No washing, no scrubbing, no cleaning or picking or peeling or emptying or nothing of that kind. All right?'

Jack nodded again, hope making his heart *moon-big.*

The pointer finger folded, then it turned and *jabbed* at Jack's chest. 'Last of all, you might ...' she looked at the dirt, her toe digging in it, 'you might teach me some of the things that you know, so I might know them, too.' She lifted her chin. 'I've a feeling, when I'm a woman of the world, when I am a woman of the circus, that knowing things might be useful.'

Jack felt his mouth open. He was meant to be learning from Angeline. She was meant to help him find his calling. He wasn't supposed to be teaching her.

And *yet* ...

If it made her like him more. If it made her his friend ...

Jack nodded, cleared his throat and said, 'I'll teach you about birds and the stars. I'll teach you *everything*.'

Angeline grinned, finally, and her teeth were crooked fence posts, but they were somehow more angelic with it. 'Good,' she declared, and then said, 'Optional extras to this pact include puddings and songs and dancing and talking about ...' she leaned in, eyes wide, 'the circus, of course!'

She smiled wider, spreading out her arms like wings and Jack could *see* it. He could *see* the glowing thing within her, again. She was special. She was a dream thing.

'I *am* going to join the circus, Jackdaw!' she cried to him and to the moon. Above her, birds – awed or frightened by her, or both – beat at the sky with their wings, turning it to a membranophone. 'I am going to be an acrobat. I am going to be a lion. I am ... well, I don't know yet what my talent will be, but it will be magnificent. I will bite holes in the tent and make everyone afeared and awondered, and I do not give two ripe figs if those ain't words, Jack Hollow, because they are words to *me* and who cares if you use words that are wrong-about as long as a person knows what you mean.'

Her wings drifted back to her sides. She held out her hand. When he took it, it was warm.

'Come with me?' she asked. 'Join me? Watch me be wild and magnificent.'

And of course, he, Jack Hollow (though he knew *nothing* of the thing he was joining – only that it was with her), both afeared and awondered, said, 'Yes.'

The burned-toast sky was buttering itself, now, turning into daylight.

'Your name?' Jack asked Angeline.

'Angeline, but you know that.'

'Your other name, I mean, like mine is *Hollow*.'

Angeline shrugged and did a little twirl and she replied, 'Neveryoumind.'

She didn't look, then, at all to Jack like a girl who needed saving, like Nell had said she was.

But looks can be deceiving.

'I'll be off,' she said. 'Lest Mrs Bristleroad have my guts for garters.' She groaned, long and loudly. She turned on her battered shoe heel and, making barely a sound, she danced away into the twilight.

Jackdaw watched the space she had left. It seemed to glisten a little, as if some marvellous spell had been cast by the mere fact of her presence.

He looked up at the sky. Crows circled, black cinders against the glow of the dawn. And then they flew away.

8
Angharad

'What are you doing, funny Jack Hollow, before the day breaks?'

Jack stood, frozen, in the middle of the Direleafe lawns, his hands held up like kangaroo paws and his legs bent mid-sneaking-stride. He turned only his head.

Angharad stood with her back against a tree, eating an enormous red apple. Her hair was a mess of curls, poorly controlled by broken hairpins. 'Don't tell,' she said. She nodded at the apple. 'It looked the most beguiling of the lot.'

Jackdaw couldn't help smiling, though his heart was beating like hummingbird wings.

Angharad always made him smile, especially when she used unexpected words like *beguiling.*

'If you won't tell about the apple, I won't tell about you sneaking away in the middle of the night,' she said, when Jackdaw didn't say anything.

'I won't tell,' he promised.

She smiled. 'Is it a girl?' she asked. 'Were you sneaking out for a girl, Jack Hollow?'

Jackdaw shook his head automatically. Because it was true. It was not a girl in the way she meant. Jack didn't like girls in *that* way. He didn't like Angeline like that – like knights and queens and star-crossed lovers.

'Good,' said Angharad, laughing. 'Because all the girls I know are in this hall and they're asleep in their beds. And besides, you should be concentrating on learning your pie-baking, not making eyes at Direleafe girls.'

'I'm not,' Jack promised. 'I'm not making eyes at any girls.'

Angharad smiled, softly. 'Well, now,' she

said. She nodded at Jackdaw as she took another bite. 'Anyhow, Master Hollow, I'll let you creep back into your little cottage there and I won't say a word. So long as you stay awake in your lessons and so long as you promise me ... you're well. In your heart and your head, like.'

Jackdaw smiled. 'I'm well,' he said. 'I'm just ...' He took a chance and confided – he could trust her. 'I'm just ... trying something new.'

Angharad winked. 'Well, I'll be, Jackdaw Hollow. I'm quietly impressed with that. I'll leave you be, then. Be sure and be quiet. Don't wake your mother. I have an appointment with the remainder of this apple and perhaps a handful of currants, too. I'm glad to see you being wild, Jackdaw. Spread your wings and see if you fly.'

Jack smiled and shivered a little.

Was this what flying felt like, then?

Was this living?

★

An hour or a moment later, Jackdaw awoke again to find Mrs Beekman on the end of his bed. She peered at him, her head inclined.

'What is it?' he asked, sitting upright as a poker. In his mind, worries jostled against each other like fighters in a ring.

She knows! She saw me!

I have let her down.

She will cast me out because she sees me, now, for who I really am – a boy, wrongly alive, not special and without a calling.

The universe's mistake.

But his mother smiled when he asked his question. Surely she would not have smiled had she *seen*, had she *known.*

Still, though.

Still the prey-birds circled.

'You've gone so pale, Jackdaw Hollow,' a voice whispered in his ear.

Nell.

And then there was giggling.

He tried to ignore it, but she continued.

'Look at your face! You're petrified!'

'Shush!' he hissed.

His mother's smile dropped.

'Never mind me,' said Jackdaw, quickly. 'I was ... still half in dreaming.'

His mother nodded. Though she did not seem entirely convinced.

'I had a dream, too,' she said. 'About a small, pale-faced girl, with a black bird on her shoulder ...' She shook her head. 'Very odd ...'

Jack cleared his throat. He repeated, 'What is it? Why are you here so early? Is it school time already?'

Mrs Beekman shook her head. 'No, dear boy. I have a message for you, from Angharad. She wishes to see you in the kitchen if you have a moment to spare before lessons. Something about puddings, I think.' She smiled. 'She likes you.'

'I like her, too,' said Jackdaw.

'She might be a good friend,' Mrs Beekman pushed.

Jack nodded. 'Yes, she would,' he said.

And it was true – he liked Angharad and Angharad liked him. He thought of her, eating that red apple. Perhaps she would make a very good friend, in time, but for now he only had space in his head for Angeline and callings.

Meeting Angeline, the night before, in the tulip field under the stars had convinced him. Assured him. She was so certain of herself and her path. She would help him to see his.

He itched to go to her now, but he knew she would not be in the tulip field. She would be back at Threadneedle House, with Mrs Bristleroad.

Was she the one Nell meant? The one who menaced Angeline?

Something inside him twisted when he thought of Angeline being mistreated. He wished he could help ... but Florence had forbade him from saving Angeline.

And a person *was not* a calling.

★

In the kitchen, Angharad presented him with a basket of lemons, and she said to him, 'Won't these make a *fine* little pudding?'

Jackdaw agreed, of course. He did his best. He *really* did.

But the pudding turned to coal, as always, while his mind drifted to fairy-wrens and caterpillars and chrysalises and the life cycles of stars.

And on again to Angeline.

'Never mind,' said Angharad, kindly, as they stood before the oven. 'There's always next time. While we are alive, Jackdaw Hollow, the world is positively brimming with next times.'

9
Unruly brains

The next night, Jack sat on the roof of Direleafe Hall. Again, three ghost girls sat beside him, but this time he could see them.

They were trying to persuade him to visit Angeline and he, suddenly and inexplicably, found himself unable to do so. His whole body vibrated with anxiety and fear.

He knew she would not come.

He imagined her absence like a hole, cut roughly in the sky, ragged-edged, as if some great hand had dropped down from the heavens and chopped her out with sewing scissors.

He imagined a flattened patch, where tulips had bowed before her, before she disappeared.

He didn't let himself imagine her *being there*. He couldn't because the hope inside him was so bright and burning. Sometimes, it's better to dim a hope than have it extinguished for us.

Quite apart from the fact that he found himself *liking* her, despite or because of her chaos and wildness ...

He felt it, so close, his calling. She would teach him how to know himself and what it was he lived for. She would teach him how to be, entirely – perfectly Jackdaw Hollow. The universe would be set to rights, soon enough, soon enough.

But only if she was there.

Hope was an aching thing within him, a thing with claws, not feathers. It could scratch, if it wanted to.

It took a minute or two of sitting and staring at the stars for Jack to realise that Nell was speaking to him.

He inclined his head. 'I'm sorry,' he said. 'I didn't hear you talking.'

Nell rolled her eyes. 'I'm well used to *that.* I'm a ghost.'

Jack shook his head. 'I go inside myself,' he said. 'I lose myself in there.'

Florence, beside Nell, leaned closer. 'How *fabulous,*' she said.

'Fabulous?' asked Jack, bemused. '*Some* might call it a failing. Disappearing from the world and into my own brain. My ... mostly unruly brain.'

Florence shook her head, vehemently. 'Not a failing. Not a power. But *fabulous*, nonetheless. Bodies are fabulous,' she said. 'You only realise it when you don't have a proper one any more. But all the quirks and foibles of *live* bodies are fascinating to me now. I love the ones that have parts that work differently. I love your strange, unruly brain, Jack Hollow. I wish I could cut it from your head and examine it and ...'

Florence realised her companions were staring at her. 'Did I go too far?' she asked.

'Always,' said Nell.

'My mother says I should view it with positivity,' said Jack, lifting a shoulder. 'My brain works differently, is all, and sometimes I like it – I like my imagination. But sometimes it prevents me from being all I want to be. Like now. Now, I feel paralysed, and it is all the fault of my brain.'

'Perhaps,' said Florence, shrugging, 'every part of us – the working parts and those that work differently – form us into the person we are. When I was living, I had one aching knee. It meant I never did running races. I sneaked to the science laboratory instead. Perhaps I would have been brilliant, still, without that aching knee, but who knows? It was *part of me*, just as your queer little brain is *part of you*, Jack Hollow. Just a piece and a piece to be proud of, I should think.'

'Did you know that Mr Michelangelo had a

brain a bit like yours?' asked Lucy, shyly. 'The painter, like? At least, I believe so. He was mighty shy and would hide himself inside, too afeared to venture out. And look what he made – look how many people he gave his wisdom to. And his paintings! They are wondrous. I think—'

'Enough, Lucy!' Nell barked. 'And you too, Florence.'

Lucy kicked at the tiles. 'I was only going to say I think Jack is wondrous, too,' she mumbled.

'That's all the way past of the point of anything,' said Nell, crossly. 'All of this sideways talk takes us further away from what *I* was saying.'

Jack looked at the night-birds that hopped across the rooftop. He allowed himself to sidle closer, but he was too eager, too noisy. They took flight and disappeared.

'What were you saying, Nell?' he asked, trying hard to keep the misery from his voice.

'I was asking if you like surprises,' she said, folding her arms.

‘I ... don’t know,’ said Jack, biting his lip. ‘I don’t honestly think I’ve encountered many, up until this point. Aside from the lightning, of course, but I don’t really remember that. After that, my mother thought it best to keep surprise far away from me. Either that or it’s just the function of living in a place such as Direleafe Hall. Latin follows mathematics, and science follows after, and then it’s lunchtime, which is usually potatoes. I don’t mind it. Within those *known* things, there are always *unknowns,* such as unexpected pardalotes. And I ...’ Jack’s brow furrowed. ‘What?’ he said to the girls who were staring.

And then he saw her, far off in the tulip field. In her white dress, she might have been a bird, or she might have been an angel.

And seeing her, *seeing* her, made him almost lose his breath.

‘There’s your surprise,’ said Nell, softly. ‘She has come.’

10

Returning to Angeline

She was so pale in the moonlight, and so made of only bones and skin. He thought, strangely, of Angharad, who was pink-cheeked and strong. This girl – this Angeline – looked like the centre of a feather, as if she might break in a rowdy wind.

She certainly looked like a girl in need of saving.

But a girl is not a calling.

And her chin was high, and her shoulders were square, like a girl in need of saving but not in want of it.

'Well, then?' she asked, tapping her foot.

Her stockinged toes could be seen through holes in the leather. 'Why are you late, so?'

He pointed to his temple.

'Do you have a gammy one?' she asked, touching her own head.

'Not gammy,' said Jack, slowly. 'Just not the *same*.'

Angeline raised an eyebrow. 'That wouldn't work at all in the circus,' she said. She raised her hands to the sky. 'You've got to be quick as a whip.'

'I'm sure it could be done,' said Jack. His voice trailed off at the end. He did not know what else to say. He only knew that she looked even more like an angel, up close. She looked like his salvation.

'You're an angel,' Jack whispered.

Angeline's dark eyebrows arched. 'I am not, neither,' she said, 'and I wouldn't want to be. Angels don't join the circus. No, I am a thing that's *bursting*, see?'

Jack didn't. Not really.

Angeline nodded. 'Life is *so* either dreary or dire. It's been that way for me, forever. I've been stuck in Threadneedle House, *surviving*, eating the gruel of life, if you like, while folks who don't deserve it, like Mrs Bristleroad, are eating life's pudding. I'm ready to eat the pudding of life, Jackdaw Hollow. You've come at just the perfect time.'

Jack looked at Angeline, captivated. It was true, he had come at the perfect time – but the perfect time for him to find his own pudding.

'Are you ready to watch me, Jack?' she said. 'Go on. Be my audience. *See* me.'

And with that she was off at a sprint, before Jack could think what to do about it, before he remembered that he too had feet and his own feet could run.

He shook himself. 'Go, you numpty!' he muttered, and he took off apace. He raced after Angeline, fighting all the way against the urge to yell at her, *Don't run so fast! You're a feather! You're only bones! You'll do yourself a tragedy!*

Finally, they found themselves in the middle of an open field.

'Watch me,' said Angeline. 'I'm going to try an *aerial somersault*.'

She tried. All legs and arms and bones and curses, she *tried*. But it reminded Jackdaw of how he tried to make apple tarts, how he tried to make plum pies and lemon puddings. Every trick Angeline tried only ended up in cinders.

That windmill stunt he'd seen her perform seemed to be an anomaly.

He felt his heart sinking, further, further. Surely, with all this failure, Angeline would soon give up on her calling to join the circus. And how could she teach him to find his, then?

But the most curious thing occurred, as Angeline tripped and stumbled. At the end of each ill-fated stunt, Angeline turned to look at him, and her angel face was so bewitching with its joy that all his misgivings fell away like snow shaken from feathers.

It was as if failure did not trouble her at all. She simply kept on trying and she seemed delighted by it all. Even the falling. Even the bruises.

As they recovered from the chaos, she said, 'Now that's done, Jack Hollow, won't you tell me all you know about pardalotes, then? I think pardalotes could be useful, in a circus.'

Jack simply nodded and didn't know how to say to her as she sat in the dirt, *You're meant to be teaching me, Angeline, and all you're teaching me is how to fall.*

11
Teachings

He taught her, first, to read.

'I might need to read in the circus,' she said. 'I might need to read my fan letters.'

Of course, Angeline could read a little bit, before this. She could read her own name and the name of her household and simple words, like *brush* and *clean* and *pudding*. She could read *circus* and *tent* and *acrobat*.

But Jack taught her more words than these. He wanted to teach her the beauty he saw when he read the perfect sentence.

In a makeshift, night-time classroom at the edge of the tulip field they sat together, a gas lamp for light when the light from the moon was not enough. She turned a tulip stem around and around in her grubby, crackled fingers, and he could not help feeling that her fingers were more perfect than the petals she held.

'Teach me *aurora*,' she whispered to him, and he spelled it out and she repeated it.

'Teach me *solace*. Teach me *serenity*,' she asked him, remembering words he'd told her before.

He wanted to say to her, more than ever, 'Please teach me your beauties as well. Teach me how you know yourself. Teach me to find my calling. You said you would teach me ... something, at least.'

But all he did was watch her tumble.

All he did was teach her to spell *serendipity*.

She leaned forwards, her eyes like fizzing water. 'Teach me to write those words, too, Jackdaw Hollow. I'll need to write back to my fans.'

And so, he showed her. He guided her hand.

She flinched away from his touch at first and snapped at him, 'Don't you place your hands on me!'

'I'm sorry,' he replied. 'I don't know how else to teach you. You do it by feel, you see.'

She nodded, slowly. 'Like cartwheels,' she said.

'Like cartwheels, exactly.'

'Go on, then,' she whispered.

'I want to teach you to write beautifully,' he said. 'It isn't worth writing if you don't do it beautifully.'

They practised together, with his hand on hers, and then her fingers alone, until it was almost beautiful.

I wish I could see a thylacine, she wrote. *I wish I could be a fox.*

After a while, he grew restless, watching her slow and careful printing. He wished for her attention.

'Could you teach me something now?' he

asked. 'Tell me ... how did you know that you wished to join the circus?'

She looked up and met his eyes. 'Can you think of anything more magnificent?' she said. She sighed, her eyes glazing. 'We only get one life,' she told him. 'Why shouldn't it be magnificent?'

'Quite,' said Jackdaw, 'but how did you know?'

She scowled at him. 'You're bothering me,' she growled and crossed her arms.

'I'm sorry,' Jack said, and he meant it. The last thing he wanted was to bother Angeline. 'Why don't I try something different? Tell me ... do you know any Latin?'

'I don't like it,' she told him, with folded arms, as he attempted to show her the word for *sorrow*. 'It sounds like boring old men and it will be of little to no use to me in the circus.'

Jack felt his stomach drop, then. Something like disappointment stuck its claws into his soul, and he did not quite know why.

The circus thing was the whole reason why he was meeting with Angeline. That was her calling and he was to find his, through learning how callings work.

But he couldn't help feeling, every time she mentioned the circus, that a little speck of dust rolled around his insides, collecting parts of himself and making itself bigger. And as the speck of dust – of disappointment – grew, his heart shrank. It became a fig again.

Perhaps it was because now he realised, truly, that to join the circus meant to *leave.*

He had only known Angeline for less than the life of a meal moth, and yet he found himself bound to her in ways he could not describe.

The ghost girls were right. He wanted Angeline to be his friend. And just as the dust mote of disappointment grew, so another – less charitable – emotion grew with it.

A hope that was not the good kind.

A hope that was cruel.

The hope that … perhaps it would never happen.

For one thing, Angeline was terrible at each act she tried to perfect. For another, this circus thing was only a distraction, surely – a shield she put around herself when life at Threadneedle House got too hard.

If he saved her, she would not need the shield.

But Florence had forbade him.

A person was not a calling, and Angeline was certainly not the sort of girl who wanted saving. If he even offered to carry her basket, she whacked him on the arm.

He tried to squash his mean little hope down, but it was terribly hard. Now, after so many years of being alone, he found that he wanted a friend like Angeline, more than all the hot cocoa in the world. Maybe all friendships were this way – like rocks in your pockets and wings on your back all at once.

He didn't know. He had only ever had Angeline.

Maybe he could find other friendships like this, if Angeline did become an acrobat. Maybe Angharad would transform from kitchen tutor to something closer.

But for now, he wanted Angeline only ... perhaps even more than he wanted his calling. His heart was a fig as she learned *trapeze* and *spectacle* and *calliope*.

But she glowed from within, and he felt so greedy and self-seeking when she glowed like that, because the glowing rubbed off on him, a little bit, and that was why he did it – that was why he did *all* of this. Because of what Angeline's glowing did to *him*.

He wished he could be happy, when she spoke of the circus. He wished he cared only for her heart and not his. He wished he could shake the feeling that all he was destined for, after all, was to sit here in the refracted glow of Angeline.

A girl is not a calling.

How disappointed Mrs Beekman would be. How disappointed his parents would have been, and the old man who found him and even that poor, lost bird he sought.

A girl is *not* a calling, and being in Angeline's glow was not enough for him to have survived.

'What's going on in that strange, feathery head of yours?' asked Angeline as his mind floated skywards.

'Nothing and nonsense,' he said, and he tried to look like he meant it.

'Liar,' she said, and she pinched him on the arm, and he treasured the bruise. It was a reminder, in the hours when he wasn't with her, that she existed.

And even if he was failing at all but adoring her, the adoring was something. At least it was feeling.

He was happy. He was happy with Angeline, even though he only watched her tumble and taught her pretty words.

He was only ever sad at the end of the night, watching her return to Threadneedle House. He saw how cold she was in those ragged clothes.

And then there was Mrs Bristleroad. She was the shadow hanging over everything in Angeline's world. At first, she seemed reticent to speak of her, shaking her head. 'No more of that monster,' she growled, when Jack asked.

But one night she arrived trembling and, when Jack asked why, she folded her arms, looking away, blinking.

Tears.

Jack, somehow, had never thought of tears when he imagined Angeline. She was doing her best to hide them but not well enough.

'She called me *nothing*,' Angeline whispered. 'She said I had no future. That I come from nothing and that nothing is what I will return to.'

'Why do you care at all what she thinks?' Jack asked her.

'I don't.'

But there had been tears. And still she was trembling.

'I don't care if she calls me stupid. Or if she

chastises me for singeing curtains or spilling lamp oil or sneaking the odd biscuit or two. But I am not nothing. I am something. Someone. And I have a future bigger than the sky.'

'You do,' Jack said. 'I know you do. She knows nothing. Why are you crying for the sake of her?'

'Because she is the only person anything like a mother that I have now,' Angeline said, in a voice so quiet that the wind almost swept it away. She looked up, suddenly, and her eyes widened.

Jack turned. A flash of white caught his vision. A woman, like an osprey, in the distance. He looked back at Angeline. 'Her?'

She nodded. 'I have to go.'

'Why? Why do you *care*?' Jack asked again.

Angeline's jaw clenched. 'You don't know what she will do to me.' Then, without another word, she took off.

Jack watched her disappear into the darkness and he knew, now, fully, what Nell had meant. Angeline needed him. Not only to be her audience. Not only to teach her big words. To save her.

He knew she had big dreams of the circus. But Jack read enough books to know that running away to the circus was simply a version of finding a door to another world.

It wasn't real.

It was smoke and mirrors and magic. Angeline dreamed of being a tumbler the way other children dream of transforming into birds. Everyone wants to fly away, in one way or another.

But it's not real. Not flying like that – like birds or acrobats.

Angeline needed a salvation that was real if Mrs Bristleroad was all that Angeline said she was.

What if the circus was not the only way that she could be free? What if there was another salvation?

Florence had warned him not to interfere,

but she hadn't seen Angeline trembling like that.

You don't know what she will do to me ...

A person was not a calling. A girl was not a calling. And he would still find his own one – he would – but wouldn't it be nicer if he found it alongside Angeline? If she stayed? If he found his calling just as she found a new one?

And then these moments with Angeline – sweet and wild and golden – could last forever.

★

Even in the moments when he was not with Angeline, still the world seemed more golden. He felt more *able* to do other things. More able to read and write and, well ... not to bake, but he enjoyed the process more, even as he burned everything still. He enjoyed watching the stars more, knowing that they watched him and saw that he was doing well. He enjoyed watching birds more and he was getting better at it. More confident. He edged closer to them and they did not fly away.

He began to draw them and he liked the way his drawings looked.

Perhaps this was how it always felt, when your heart opened to a thing. It opened, at the same time, to everything.

12
Eavesdropping

There were no storm clouds this day at Direleafe Hall. The sunlight was the colour of Colman's mustard and the air smelled of wattle and just-cut grass.

Jack Hollow sat on the roof, again, contemplating.

He watched birds and they watched him back and, sometimes, when a bird flew down, down and towards him, he allowed himself to move a little bit more closely and just observe it. And it observed him. There was communion in this. He still worried it would fly away, but he enjoyed this moment, too. This communion.

Jack Hollow was spending more and more time up on the roof. It was a good place for thinking. It was a good place for making *plans*. For himself and his life and, yes, plans for how to help Angeline.

But Florence warned you ... She said Angeline would not want it ...

Jack's mind kept looping back to this. He wanted to do what Angeline wanted. He did not want to do anything that pushed her away, or made her think less of him.

But Mrs Bristleroad called her nothing ...

The roof was also a good place for emptying his mind of all of it. For simply watching the birds and the sky.

Sometimes, he wished that this – this being with birds and the breeze on his cheeks – could be the calling he searched for. Sometimes, he wished that laughing with Mrs Beekman could be, while drinking hot cocoa under their favourite black blanket. That baking pies with Angharad could be.

That running through the tulips with Angeline could be.

But callings had to be big, didn't they? A lightning bolt was big. A calling had to be just as big as that.

Eventually, daylight dimmed, and Jack's belly began to grumble and his thoughts turned to pies. He didn't wish to make one – not this time. He wanted something edible, not charcoal in a vaguely pie-like shape. He wished for one of Angharad's pies.

But when he came to the kitchen door, he heard voices on the inside. He pressed himself against a wall and listened.

He heard Mrs Beekman say, 'Do you think I'm failing my Jack? Is my *bringing up* of him wanting, somehow?'

Angharad replied, 'Whatever do you mean? He is a credit to you, Mrs Beekman. He may be a woeful baker, but he's clever and kind and respectful. And certain, he's not a *usual* boy, perhaps ... is that what you mean? Is that why you worry? Because *usual*, I think, is not the thing we should be striving for in life.'

'You're ever wise, Angharad,' said Mrs Beekman. 'And I would not change one hair on that boy's head. But ... I do wonder sometimes if keeping him here at Direleafe Hall might be damaging. He's up on that roof again, staring at clouds. He seems so weary these days, as if he's hardly sleeping at all. He's ever yawning in lessons, his eyes on the window instead of the chalkboard. Am I doing him a disservice, bringing him up here? I do wonder if ... it breaks my heart to even think it, but ... perhaps I should send him to the boys' school over yonder, so he can experience *other boys* and perhaps make a proper friend ...'

Jack's heart stopped.

'Oh, no,' said Angharad. 'He'd have learned some much harsher lessons, long ago, if he were at a school for young men. In my experience, some boys can be especially cruel to souls like Jack Hollow. I think he's just fine here, Mrs Beekman, and he'll find his way in the world when it's time. Sometimes, it just takes a little longer. He'll find his purpose soon as springtime.'

As she said this, a tiny sparrow flew through the window and landed on her shoulder. She did not brush it off. It stayed there, happy in her company.

'Thank you, Angharad,' said Mrs Beekman. 'I know in my heart of hearts that it's true – Jack belongs here and he's happy enough – but it's the cruelty of being a mother. This constant, scritch-scratching voice in your ear, declaring, *You're doing it poorly! You'll make a mess of him!*'

Angharad laughed. 'Oh, Mrs Beekman,' she said. 'We're all messes, aren't we? What matters is we're happy messes and all it takes for a child to be happy is to have someone who *cares* about how well or poorly they're doing it. All that matters, really, is to have someone who cares at all.'

'I want the world for him,' Mrs Beekman

said, sadly. ‘I want that boy to have the whole, wide world.’

Jack pushed himself away from the wall, then, and tiptoed up to his room. Inside his soul, there was a storm, a hurricane.

He could not bear the thought of his mother wishing to send him away. This place ... it was his home. The only home he’d ever known. He was not like Angeline. He did not wish for circuses. He wished for his mother and hot cocoa and the birds on the Direleafe roof.

But your calling must be bigger than cocoa and birds ...

Jack knew it, but still ...

But *still* ...

And then there was the idea that his mother wished more for him than what he was – small and shy and nervous and *not-usual.*

She wished for him to have the whole, wide world. That must be her way – surely – of saying his calling must be grand and enormous – *whole-wide-world big.*

Jackdaw knew it – his calling must be enormous – but still, he felt frightened. He wanted to please his mother, but he still didn't know how. All he had was a half-baked idea of how to save a girl.

Would that be enough?

Jackdaw thought of Mrs Beekman taking him in under her wing when his birth parents died. Perhaps saving Angeline in the way Mrs Beekman had saved him would be enough to show her that she wasn't making a mess of anything.

But Florence ...

The emptiness in Jack's belly was gone, now. He no longer thought of pies. All thoughts of pies had been replaced with one question:

What should I do?

Suddenly, the stars and the night-birds seemed to call to him. He could hear her voice drawing him out and away and into the dark, too.

Angeline.

Jack wasn't tired, now, but he'd have to hide his yawns in the morning. He could do that. He could pretend he wasn't weary, so his mother wouldn't worry.

After all, this is what his mother wanted.

He was off into the world, to find out how to make his bigger.

★

She was there, waiting, the fire in her eyes as bright as always.

There was only a fingernail moon in the sky. There were not so very many stars. His mind and soul were so full of *everything*, he didn't notice her face at first.

At first.

The night-birds saw, though.

The bruises beneath her eyes were the colour of ink and plums. They might have been beautiful, coloured like that. But Jackdaw Hollow knew better.

13
Bruises

Angeline turned her face towards the sky. Beneath the moon-glow, the bruises were purple as flax lily, as blue as midsummer sky.

All the questions inside Jack's soul disappeared. No longer did he think, *What should I do?* No longer did he think of Florence's warning.

'Who did it?' Jack asked, his jaw tight as a Palomar knot. His body was no longer flesh and blood and skin and bone but *rage.* He vibrated with it. Every hair on his head was taut with it.

She said nothing, only crossed her arms

over that ratty woollen shawl. In the dirt, her toe carved the shape of a star.

'Your eyes,' Jack said, as if it could be anything else. 'Your eyes – who ... blackened them?'

'Not black,' Angeline muttered, her chin jutting defiantly. 'I rather think they're *indigo*.' She looked up, finally, and Jack saw that her eye whites were mercury-silver, the tears catching the moonlight like so many tiny, awful mirrors. She didn't even try to hide it, this time.

'Was it her?' Jack whispered.

Angeline nodded, ever-so-slightly. Just the tiniest of jerks. 'She is a monster,' she said.

'Has she ... hit you before?' Jack asked.

Angeline nodded. 'Often and always. It's all well, though. I am running, soon. All the way to the circus and she will never touch me again.'

Jack shook his head. 'The circus is only fancy and pretend,' he said. 'Come with me. Come to Direleafe Hall. Mrs Beekman would let you live there, I'm sure.'

Angeline shook her head, fiercely. 'I can't run to Direleafe Hall. I can't leave and go only through the tulip patch. I can only leave if I run and run, all the way to the circus. It's my *dream.* It has been since forever, since even before my parents died. They loved to watch me, Jackdaw, and I can't help thinking, perhaps, if I joined the circus ... they might come and watch me there, again.'

Jack shook his head, thinking of what Nell had told him. 'They can't. When you die, you're fixed to a place. They won't be able to come to the circus.'

Angeline's expression darkened. 'You don't know that, Jack. You don't know anything.'

'Come to Direleafe,' Jack pleaded. 'We could have such a grand time there, together. I could teach you more – I like teaching you. And you could find other callings ...'

Angeline huffed. 'I don't *want* another calling. And I can't run only to the hall. It's too close. She would find me. She would bring me straight back to Threadneedle and ... if she gives me these bruises for such small things, imagine what she would do if I did something *enormous* like that! She would break me, entirely, if I did that. The only way I could ever run to Direleafe Hall is if Mrs Bristleroad was gone.' Her voice lowered. 'She really would break me, Jackdaw.'

Angeline crouched down and began tracing in the dirt with her finger.

'No,' Jack said, and he put his hand, lightly, on Angeline's moon-haloed hair. 'You will not be broken. I will not allow it.'

Angeline looked up at him, all of a sudden. His hand dropped away, and he thought, for one heartbeat-halting moment, that she might whisper to him, *Thank you*, or even, *My hero*, the way girls sometimes did in books.

Instead, her eyes sparked and glowered, like they had on that first night, and she said to him, 'Jack Hollow, you can march yourself all the way to *blazes*!'

She stood and began marching herself – to

blazes or elsewhere, he didn't know which – and Jack called after her, 'Where are you going? What did I *say*?'

Angeline stopped, but she did not turn. 'My life is not yours to meddle with, Jackdaw Hollow. I am in charge of my *own* salvation.'

'Wait!' Jack said as she began to leave him.

She did not wait.

'Let me help,' Jack said, but of course she did not hear.

He again thought, *What should I do?* and he thought of Florence's warning. Finally, he thought of Thelma and Henry Hollow, his birth parents, and how he had been only a babe when they died – too young to save them.

He was not a babe, now. And he might not be the strongest of boys, nor the bravest, but he could be a hero. For Angeline, he could.

He had to. He could not allow her to be broken.

14
Tulips and thistles

Jackdaw Hollow was good at learning. At Direleafe Hall, he was renowned, not only as the sole boy but also as a boy who studied well and knew things. Jackdaw Hollow knew how to prepare for examinations. He knew how to research his assignments. It was nothing like a calling – this ability to retain information. But it could be useful.

It would be useful in this – this plan. His plan to save Angeline.

'What is he doing?' Lucy asked Florence as they watched the boy, far off in the tulip field. He was not with Angeline, this evening.

But he was near her. Observing her.

'I think,' said Florence, 'that he is doing something silly.'

'You think he means to save her?' asked Lucy.

'I think he means to try,' sighed Florence. 'I did attempt to warn him.'

'Perhaps it will all be well,' said Nell, chewing her lip.

Florence shook her head. 'I think, Nell, that this "saving" business is going to be Jackdaw Hollow's cherry tree.'

Nell winced. She remembered the fall. She remembered well what it felt like to know all was lost. She hoped very much that she had not delivered the same fate to Jackdaw Hollow.

Florence sighed, disapprovingly. 'And all this,' she said, 'because you wished to be seen.'

Nell opened her mouth to protest and then closed it. After all, what could she say? Florence was completely right. Much as Nell detested it, she almost always was.

★

Jack watched Angeline, for an hour or more, as she cartwheeled and sang and walked a bedsheet tightrope. He liked it best when she danced. He felt something, deep inside him, like birds taking flight, when she danced.

He watched her and he thought – he *hoped* – that watching her might give him a notion of what to do. But it wasn't until he was caught that the idea was gifted to him in glorious happenstance.

'Jackdaw Hollow, you think I can't see you there?'

Jack winced.

He popped his head up and gave her a clumsy little wave. 'Hellooo!' he called out, then immediately regretted the strange, warbling sound of his voice.

She stomped over to him.

'So, let me get this all together,' she said, tersely. 'I'm out here, waiting for you to show your feathery head, and the whole time you *were* here but hiding? What are you *doing*, you strange little creature?'

'You ... were waiting for me?' Jack whispered.

Angeline nodded, curtly. 'I need my audience. And ... I thought you might teach me something this night, about superstitions.'

'Superstitions?' Jackdaw asked. 'Like rabbit's feet and black cats and such?'

Angeline flopped onto the ground next to him. He noticed, then, that she had a new scratch on her arms. He touched her skin, lightly, with his finger. It was ice-chest cold. 'Mrs Bristleroad?' he asked.

'Not this time,' she said, rolling her big eyes. 'I climb out a window, you see, to come here. It's the only window in the house that won't lock. A piece of wood came sharp and loose and, well, scratches.'

The only window ... Jack thought, the words catching in his mind like yarn on a twig. *Won't lock* ...

'Anyhow,' said Angeline, '*superstitions.* I heard one of the scullery girls say the word about Mrs Bristleroad. Black cats and rabbit's feet and all of it, apparently, and I do remember – once – she got terribly cross at me for opening a parasol inside. And another time, now I remember, she threw a currant bun at Mr Hardbread for opening a ladder right where she might walk under it. What do you know of superstitions, Jackdaw Hollow?'

Jack lifted his shoulder. 'As much as you do, I'd wager. Superstitions have been around since the dawn of man, and it's not only man who practises them.'

'Women, too,' said Angeline, darkly.

'Quite. But anyhow, pigeons are quite superstitious, did you know? And superstitions themselves, in humans, tend to come from fear. Or ignorance.'

'I don't believe Mrs Bristleroad is afraid of anything,' said Angeline.

'Everyone is, a bit,' said Jack.

'I'm not,' said Angeline. 'Except for ...' she looked off into the distance, '... except for forever,' she said, finally. 'This being forever,

I mean. Being at Threadneedle House forever. That scares me.'

'That won't happen.'

Angeline glanced at him. 'I know. I won't let it.'

'Neither will I.'

He thought that Angeline's eyes might soften. He should have known better by now.

She shook her head. 'You never learn, do you, Jack Hollow?'

'I do,' he replied. And then, quietly, to himself, he added, 'I've learned almost all I need to know tonight.'

Angeline didn't hear him. She was busy singing a strange song below her breath. Something about *hatchlings.*

He reached down and plucked a tulip from the dirt. He didn't say, *You're as pretty as a tulip to me.* He hoped that the tulip itself might be enough.

Angeline took it and she tucked it down the front of her moth-holed linen dress. He thought she might say, *Thank you*, but instead she bent and picked a thistle and gave it to Jack.

'I ain't a flower of the usual sort,' she told him. 'But whoever said that a tulip was better than a briar?'

Some thistle milk dripped onto Jackdaw's hand, silver and sticky.

'Mrs Bristleroad would hate that,' Angeline said, pointing. 'She hates anything that sticks or clags. And she hates thistles, too. Her favourite flower is a bluebell, the colour of her pretty, cold eyes.'

'At Direleafe Hall there are lots of thistles,' Jack said. 'On the wallpaper and such. Mrs Beekman says when the school was built, the ground was all covered in thistles and that's why they called the place Direleafe, for the prickles, I suppose. But they pulled them all up and poisoned them all and planted cherry trees and silver birches and, in the paddocks, they planted tulips.'

'Hmmm.' Angeline shook her head. 'I think

that's right. I think every one of those girls at Direleafe Hall might be a tulip. But maybe the hall itself is still a thistle.'

'Maybe that's why I like it there so much,' said Jack. 'Maybe it's why I like you. You're right. Thistles are wonderful.' He looked down at his toes. 'What would I be, if I were a flower?' he asked her.

Angeline inclined her head. 'You're not a flower, Jack Hollow,' she said. 'I consider you a bird.'

15
He'll ruin everything

'She told you not to,' said Florence.

'She specifically *said*,' added Nell.

'Did you not hear?' asked Lucy, timidly. 'I'm sure I heard her say it ...'

'This was all a mistake,' muttered Nell. 'I know it was my idea but ... I was wrong. I'm never wrong, but I was wrong, this time.'

'I did hear,' Jack said, without pausing to look at the ghosts. He was busy, now, in the kitchen, and he had his hands full.

Angharad or one of the other girls would surely be here any moment.

Jackdaw was not busy burning pies, this

time. He was busy stealing treacle and he had to do it quickly, but the ghosts would not leave him be. 'I did hear, but you weren't wrong. Sometimes people say a thing and it's not a thing they mean. I know that I—'

'Are you in here, Jack Hollow?'

Jack cursed. He tried to hide the treacle behind his back but, as he did so, the lid came askew and slopped a dollop of sticky darkness down his leg. It was warm and uncomfortable.

Angharad noticed, because of course she did. Angharad noticed everything. She raised an eyebrow and she looked so pretty, even as she judged him. Her curdle-milk curls struggled to break free from beneath her cotton bonnet. Her eyelashes above her ivy-green eyes were as pale as mealybugs.

'Nothing,' Jack blurted. 'Just, um, studying ... for ... pie-making.'

Angharad peered at him. 'I didn't ask what you were doing,' she said, simply. She gave him the ghost of a smile. 'I only asked if you were here.'

The ghost girls exchanged a look. The cooking girl was smarter than any of them.

'I'm here,' he told Angharad. 'And I really was just looking at ingredients for ... for treacle pie, of course. I think I could make a good treacle pie. Why are you? Here, I mean.'

Angharad stared at him. 'I work here.' She grinned and held up a basket. 'I have some gooseberries,' she said. 'What about a treacle-and-gooseberry pie?'

'I'd like that,' said Jack, smiling. 'Only ... not right now. I'm busy.'

Angharad's brow furrowed. 'You said you were after pie-making.'

'I ... am ... but ...'

Angharad nodded slowly. 'The gooseberries are only just ripe. They will keep.' She began to turn away but before she did, she added, 'This project ... are you certain about it?'

'What do you mean?' asked Jackdaw.

Angharad cleared her throat. 'I mean ... sometimes, we think we are doing a thing for one reason, but it's really for another. Sometimes, we think we are doing the right thing, but it's not a thing that is wanted. Or needed. Sometimes, we think a thing will make another person happy, but it's not what they want at all.'

The ghost girls exchanged another look. Had she heard? Did she know?

'Listen to her,' Florence whispered. 'You wouldn't listen to me. Listen to her.'

'What do you know of anything?' asked Jackdaw, not unkindly.

'I know,' Angharad said, turning to him, 'that you have spent your life worrying that the universe made an error in saving you and that, one day, everyone will discover it. That Mrs Beekman will discover it and turn you out. That the Direleafe girls will discover it and be cruel to you, as you believe you deserve. I know this is why you don't make friends, because you consider yourself an impostor. But I am your friend, Jackdaw Hollow, and the girls would love you, if you let them. They think you odd, yes, but they like you nonetheless. Let them love you. Let *all* of us love you. You don't have to do this ... *project* to prove anything. You are already proven.'

Jackdaw nodded, hesitantly. 'Thank you,' he croaked, his cheeks flushed and his eyes, curiously, burning.

Angharad smiled. 'It's all right,' she said. 'I suppose I'm a little bit busy, too. I saw a small kitten prowling around the grounds. I'm half a mind to catch it and make it my own.' She skipped from the room, in search of kittens.

'Listen to her,' said Nell. 'She speaks the truth. I should never have introduced you to Angeline. She's not right for you, and you're not right for her. I imagined myself doing you both a service, but I failed on all accounts.' It wasn't like Nell to admit fault. Only true desperation could make it happen.

'Stay at Direleafe Hall,' Florence implored him. 'Maybe just ... stay a little while. Think on the proper thing to do. Angeline will wait for you. Or she won't even notice. She'll be happy enough, performing cartwheels ...'

'I'm not staying,' said Jack, his chin in the air. 'No matter what you or Angharad says. I know you're all only worried, for my heart, but my heart knows itself. It is fixed. This my *calling*.'

'It's not,' said Nell. 'A person is not a calling. You haven't found your calling yet.'

'I have,' said Jackdaw.

'But what Angharad said—' Lucy began.

'What about what *Angeline* said!' Florence cried. She shook her head. 'I sound like a cicada, only ever singing the one note. The girl does not want saving! She wants to save herself. She has a *plan*, I'd wager, to do it.'

'She has no proper plan,' Jack protested. 'If she had a plan, she would have no bruises. And she gave me a thistle.' He pointed at another book on the stack beside him. 'I looked it up. Thistles symbolise noble courage and she gave the thistle to *me.* She gave it to me because she wishes *me* to be her hero!'

He stood and he walked away from the ghost girls. Florence shook her head as she watched the slender form of him disappear into the darkness of the hallway. 'I'll wager she meant that the thistle symbolised *her,*' she muttered.

'He's going to ruin everything, isn't he?' sighed Lucy.

Florence nodded. 'I told you all along,' she said. 'But nobody listens to me.'

16
Treacle

Jackdaw Hollow was excellent at learning. He knew all about the Greek gods and Henry the Eighth and Galileo and even the best way to solve most philosophical conundrums.

Jackdaw Hollow had learned all he needed to know to thwart Mrs Bristleroad and rescue Angeline. He had all the ingredients – an unlocked window, a superstitious housekeeper who hated sticky things, a jar of treacle ... The only trouble was, Jackdaw Hollow was about as good at planning as he was at baking.

The plan was to get rid of Mrs Bristleroad, so Angeline could come with him to Direleafe

Hall, and they could live together, happily and always, finding their callings side by side.

Unfortunately, Jackdaw Hollow got everything just a little bit jumbled, a little bit wrong-way-up. His plan was a pie and, like all his pies, it came out just a bit *oddways.*

Jackdaw Hollow was dressed as a cat.

Not only had he stolen the treacle, see, but his mother's favourite black woollen blanket. He had made ears from scraps of leather and a tail from a ribbon he'd found in the grass, blown out of the hair of a Direleafe girl.

He was the biggest, blackest, unluckiest cat there was.

He held a jar of the stickiest treacle possible.

And his plan was this – to creep in through the one unlocked window and sidle down the hallway until he found the bedroom of Mrs Bristleroad ...

He would then proceed to hiss and howl and, when she leaped from her bed, all aflutter and afeared, he'd pour treacle all over her head.

And then he would cry, in his best black-cat voice, *Go! Go! Away from this place, never to be seen again! Or else I shall return, the black cat of the moors, every night to haunt you!*

Jackdaw Hollow had read enough books about ghosts and the like to know how to perform a haunting.

It began as well as he had imagined – he sneaked from the Direleafe grounds and, the Midlands air cold and alive-making on his cheeks, in his lungs, he ran and ran to Threadneedle House.

There, he spotted the one cracked-open window from which Angeline had already climbed. He scaled the clay pipes that led to the roof, shimmied through the window and tiptoe-tiptoed down the grand portrait-lined hallway.

He peeped in this door and that. The gentleman of the house snored like a steam train. The kitchen girls' room smelled of cinnamon. Finally, he found a room where a woman slept, hair white and glistening as an osprey's. He tiptoe-tiptoed across to her bed and ...

The woman in the bed sat upright as a fire poker.

Then, she screamed.

And, just as Jack noticed that the woman in the bed had dark eyes, not blue, and that the white was a sleeping cap and the hair beneath it was blood red, not icy blonde ... Jack dropped his treacle pot onto those shining floorboards and it smashed like a widow's heart.

Jack Hollow's plans turned to shards of pottery from the broken jar and oozing treacle all over the floor.

And the woman who was not Mrs Bristleroad screamed, and the woman who was not Mrs Bristleroad pointed, and Jack's feet were stuck to the floor with treacle and with fear.

As Jack Hollow stood, silhouetted in the doorway, turned from boy to dark-feathered shadow, the woman yelled in a voice too fancy to ever belong to a housekeeper – a voice that could only belong, he realised, to the lady of the house – 'Help me! Mrs Bristleroad! Help me!'

And Jack finally found that his feet could move. He raced across to the bedroom window. He unlocked it just in time to hear footsteps approaching the room. He climbed through it just in time to hear a voice as cold as the winter air snap, 'That Angie girl is not in her bed, my lady. This whole mess must be her doing!'

Jack's heart cracked.

He clambered across the roof and down the pipe again, and then he was on the grass and running all the way back to Direleafe Hall.

He ran through the tulips. She was not there. She must be on her way back to Threadneedle House. He knew he should go after her, but then she would know ...

She would know what he had done. And everything would be ruined and she would hate him and there would be no calling and no forever and he would be done for, entirely.

He wiped a tear from his eye and he ran further, over the grass. He ran through the high iron gates, and the whole way his feet and his heart beat her name.

An-gel-ine. An-gel-ine. An-gel-ine.

He threw off Mrs Beekman's black blanket. He removed his leather-scrap ears. He untangled the ribbon and let it fly out his open window into the sky and away like his dreams.

He clambered into his cosy, warm bed at twelve minutes past three in the morning and he cried all the way to dawn.

17
Lies

That morning, Mrs Beekman asked Jack questions, and Jack, in answer, lied.

She asked the questions because she had heard him crying.

She had heard him crying because she had woken from a dream about a dark-haired girl and a red-haired girl and a crow who loved them both. It was a strange dream, but it felt like comfort. She had woken smiling, but then she had heard her boy – her precious heart in a boy – sobbing in his room.

She had leaped from her bed and raced to his room and pressed her hand to the door, and she wanted badly to burst in there and wrap him in her arms and her love and her favourite black blanket and make it all well again.

But something stopped her.

Something told her, *Wait.* That his tears were secret, and she should not pry. She should leave him with the ceremony of his sorrow and ask her questions later.

In the morning, it was time.

'Is there something troubling your heart?' she asked him, passing him a mug of cocoa across the breakfast table. She could not find her black blanket, but that was a worry for another time.

Jack looked up at her. His eyes were red-circled and sad. He did not answer.

She cleared her throat. 'Jackdaw, you know that no matter what befalls you, you will always have my love. No matter what and how big and how terrible it might seem, I will be here, with cocoa and a blanket ...'

She trailed off. Jack's cheeks, she noticed, reddened a little. She did not question it.

'Nothing is troubling my heart,' Jack whispered.

Mrs Beekman felt her soul flood with bewilderment and sorrow when her boy lied to her.

Jack saw her whole soul, every day.

She wished he would show her his. She wished his heart would not be broken. She wished she could pull him close, into her nest, and hold him there forever.

'I wish I could believe you, my Jack,' Mrs Beekman said. 'I want to believe you. And if I do catch you lying to me ...' She shook her head, searching for a dissuasion, a punishment that would not hurt his heart but would make him think twice. She said it not out of anger but out of desperation. It was the single thing she could think of, to keep her dear boy safe.

She hated the thought of punishing him, but if it was the only way ...

'I will make you scrub the kitchen floors, Jack Hollow, 'til they sparkle and shine. And then ... if you lie again ...'

Jackdaw looked up at her and his eyes now were spilling over with tears. 'Would you send me away?'

Mrs Beekman's breath caught like a fish in a net, and she whispered, 'Oh, my boy. You are my whole heart. I love you more than I can say. I want the world for you.'

'I want the world for me, too,' Jack murmured, lowering his forehead to his palms. 'But I am failing.'

Mrs Beekman could not stop the tears that fell from her eyes like blossoms at the end of springtime. 'My boy,' was all she could say.

She wrapped him in her arms, in her love, and she hoped it was enough.

18
You've ruined everything

Jack let his mother hold him and he wished he could feel comfort. But all he could think of was that she hadn't said *no* when he asked if she would cast him out. All he could think of was that this is what he deserved.

His plan had failed. All his plans had failed.

He had not found his calling.

He had not saved Angeline.

And she hadn't taught him anything. Nell was wrong. Angeline hadn't taught him a thing. She'd only made his heart a fig.

And now, his mother might send him away, and he deserved it. If she found out about what happened at Threadneedle House, his banishment would happen, certain as sunrise.

'How can I fix it?' he whispered to himself.

But of course, his mother still held him. Of course, his mother heard. 'I have an idea,' she told him. She pulled away. 'Jackdaw Hollow, you are so good at learning, but some of the Direleafe girls are not. Perhaps you might think of sharing what you know with them.'

Jack thought, of course, of Angeline and how he had taught her all the things he knew and all the things that set his heart on fire. He had, secretly, loved it. He never got much of a chance here at Direleafe to share his loves and fascinations. It occurred to him, now, that much as Angeline had yearned for an audience, so had he.

And yet, he shook his head. 'Teaching is not a calling.'

His mother's face froze a little. She nodded, stiffly. 'Well,' she said, 'I disagree with that, naturally. Perhaps ... perhaps you will reconsider.'

She stood, abruptly, and moved from the room, and Jackdaw felt much worse, still.

He had hurt his mother. His mother had never hurt him – not once.

And he had ruined everything.

'You've ruined everything.'

Jack turned. There was Nell, tiny but ferocious, her twig-like arms crossed over her chest, her pointed chin held high.

As soon as his mother was out of earshot, Jack glowered back at her and, even though it wasn't what he believed, but because he was filled with fury and despair that enveloped *everything*, he hissed, 'No! You've ruined everything. I was quite fine before you three came and messed everything up. Look what you did. Look what *happened*. Everything is broken. And you three did it all. But you, especially, Nell. You, especially, ruined it all.'

Nell's heart broke properly, then.

It was worse than falling from a cherry tree.

19
Hope

When the ghost girls woke Jack that night, he *harrumphed* and rolled towards the wall. 'She won't be there,' he said. 'It's impossible. She won't want to see me. Not after what I did. She won't be there, and you caused it.'

'We may have pushed you towards the friendship,' said Nell, looking away from the other girls so they wouldn't see her tears. 'That was our failing. My failing. You shouldn't ever force friendship, I think. And perhaps I tricked you, somewhat, with all that talk of destinies. She is not yours. She has her own. You and I tried to meddle in it and that was a poor choice indeed. But *you* chose the treacle, Jackdaw. You chose to *ignore* her wants and needs, and you *chose* to do this foolish thing. Let us both choose differently this time.'

'You must go to see her,' Florence said. 'First, you must check on her welfare – that she is safe from Mrs Bristleroad. Then, you must make amends for what you have done. You must apologise, Jackdaw Hollow.'

'I suppose you will tell me again now,' he said to Florence, darkly, 'that if I had listened to you, there would be no need for apologies?'

Florence shook her head. 'I was not about to say that,' she said. 'What's done is done and cannot be undone, but you must choose to atone.'

Jack growled a little. 'There will be no choosing,' he insisted. 'Because she *will not be there*.'

'But what if she is?' asked Lucy, hush-voiced and sparkle-eyed.

'What if she is and you don't come?' added

Florence. 'It's illogical not to try.'

'Do you really want to take the chance?' asked Nell. 'Go, won't you, with your heart and eyes open, instead of blundering on, stamping over all the tulips? You're *living*, Jack Hollow. *Chances* are the best thing you have, but they're not in abundance, even for you with blood and a beating heart.'

Lucy ran one cold finger down Jack's cheek. 'The hope should draw you on,' she whispered, 'even when things seem impossible. Hope should draw you on and on, Jack Hollow, and all the way to the other side. Hope is a tulip in springtime. Hope is a thistle that grows through the cracks, that grows on mountainsides, where nothing else will grow. Hope is a bird that takes flight, over and again, even though flying seems an impossible thing. Even though it's dangerous. Hope is a baby who *survives*.' She pressed a hand to Jack's chest. 'Hope is a heart that keeps loving, *over and again*, no matter how many times it is broken.'

'How did you get to know so many things?' Jack asked Lucy.

'Life teaches you,' Lucy said, gazing pink-cheeked at her toes. 'Death teaches you more. And I've only been dead a short time. In a decade more I'll be a genius.'

'You won't,' said Florence. 'I will.'

'I don't want to have to die to know things,' Jack said.

'Then just live a long life,' Florence said, matter-of-factly. 'I don't know for certain because I never did it, but I expect a long life would teach you just as much, especially if the life is a happy one.'

'You will not be happy if you always regret your actions this night,' Nell added, impatiently. 'If you always regret *not* going to see Angeline. Regretting the things that you have done is bad enough. Regretting the things that you have *not* done is far, far worse.'

Nell didn't go on, but Jack believed her. She didn't say how she knew it, but he believed.

It was not often that Nell looked sad. She did, now.

It was that sadness and the things Lucy had said and the cool tingle of Florence's hand, guiding him to stand, that convinced Jack Hollow to take the chance, choose hope and sneak out of Mrs Beekman's cottage once more.

A large part of him did not expect to find her in the middle of the tulip field. And that large part was wholly correct, but not in the way he'd imagined.

Instead, he found her standing outside the gates of Direleafe Hall.

The unexpectedness of her being there almost stopped his heart, and so did the unexpectedness of *her*. The moonlight made her an angel, shimmering. She was an angel, anyhow, without it.

'You're here,' he whispered.

'I'm here,' she said.

'I did not think you would come,' Jack told her, 'to the tulip field, let alone all the way *here*.'

'I did not think I would come at all.' She stomped her foot. 'Curse you, Jack Hollow. I should *not* have come! Do you have any inkling what my day has been like?'

Jack peered at her face. He didn't see bruises. That didn't mean there weren't any hiding beneath the sleeves of that ragged dress.

'I'm so sorry,' he said, willing his cowardly tears to stay beneath his eyelids.

Angeline's face softened a little. 'Life is too short for sorries,' she said. 'This *night* is too short for sorries. This night is a night of friendship and games.'

'Circus games?' Jack asked, fireflies in his chest.

'No,' Angeline replied. 'Games to show you the wrongness of all you have done. Now, come with me, Jack Hollow. It's the last time I will ask you.'

Jack followed her, through the Direleafe gates. Because of course he did. He would follow her to heaven or hell if he had to.

That is how Jack Hollow came to be standing, not in heaven or hell, but on the front steps of Direleafe Hall. And he held a stone in his hand.

20
The stone

Angeline, of course, was the one who gave him the stone. And when she did, his heart at first became *huge* because she had given him this small gift, this small piece of her.

But then ...

'You should throw it,' she said, pointing. 'At Direleafe Hall.'

He turned to her, mouth open. 'Why would I do that?' he asked.

She shrugged. 'For me,' she said, chin up, haughty. 'Throw the stone for me.'

His heart became a fig again.

'Don't throw it,' said Lucy.

'Don't throw it,' said Florence.

'Don't throw it!' said Nell. 'I'm warning you!'

'I don't want to throw it,' Jack said.

But part of him did. Part of him *did* because Angeline had asked him to. Part of him did because he would run to the other side of the world for her, all the way, with no shoes on. He would run to the stars. She was his purpose, his reason, and all she had done was ask him to throw one small stone.

Part of him *did* because what if this was the moment? What if this was the moment when the coin balanced on an edge, one side the favoured one, the other labelled *doom*? What if this was the moment the lightning bolt hovered in the sky, mulling, considering, *Will I hit that small, frightened family, huddled beneath that tree, or the empty ground far over there where nobody shelters?*

An enormous, noisy, persuasive part of Jack Hollow wanted to throw the stone because it would show Angeline that he was ...

Worth something.

What if he threw this stone and it was this thing that made her stay, that made her see he could be a hero, that he was strong enough to save her?

He wanted that more than anything.

Except.

Except.

Except.

'I don't want to throw it,' he repeated. He turned, slowly, to Angeline. 'Why should I throw it? Direleafe Hall is my home. It's the only home I can remember and the best home I could imagine. Mrs Beekman lives here and Mrs Beekman loves me and gives me everything and there is *no reason* why I should throw a stone.'

Angeline crossed her arms. 'You should throw the stone, Jack Hollow, because I never got to have a place like Direleafe Hall. You should throw the stone because sometimes, when we have ourselves a place that is warm and cosy and *safe* and full of love where people think we are never bad and only good, and *special*, we need to throw a *missile* at that place and *run*. I want to watch you throw this stone and then I will know that, when I am gone, you will not simply fall back into safety and comfort and a *nothing* sort of life. If you throw this stone, Jackdaw, it will set you on the path to finding your own circus. It will set you on the path to being *free*.'

Angeline's words made a kind of sense, of course, but what *if*...

What if freedom is different for everyone?

What if, for Angeline, it was running?

What if, for Jackdaw, it was finding his calling right here?

He looked up at the stars and at the night-birds as they circled and he felt an immense and all-consuming calm.

Here, right now, living. That was the best of it all.

At that exact moment, as if it were cowering in fear of Angeline's wildness, the moon hid behind a cloud. And, as Jack looked at Angeline, her silver varnish now stripped away, he didn't see an angel any more. He didn't see a dream. He didn't see a circus performer, either.

He didn't see his calling.

In one moment, both dark and light, Jack Hollow awoke.

And he *saw her.*

He saw an angry, frightened little girl. He saw a girl who didn't know how to be a friend, not properly, because the only love she'd had in her life had been torn away from her and afterwards, nobody had held her, nobody had said it would be all right. He saw a girl who had never loved him, the way he loved her, because the varnish might make her glimmer, but it also made her hard. He saw a girl who would ask him to throw a rock at a place that had done nothing to deserve it.

And maybe it was for him that she asked. Maybe she did want to set him on a path to freedom. But if that was what she wanted, then she didn't know him. Exactly as he didn't know her.

If that was the case, she thought she knew what was good for him, but it wasn't. Because he wasn't Angeline. And Angeline wasn't him. They were not alike at all.

He felt as if he had been dreaming, this whole time.

This was the thing she was meant to teach him. How lucky he was. How fortunate. Despite everything, Jackdaw Hollow was a most fortunate child. And this was his fortune and his calling, right here and now – *living*, right here and now, with cocoa and birds and the stars and his mother.

What if his calling was living and learning and reading and drinking cocoa and watching birds and just ...

Seeing.

Just seeing what happened.

His parents never got the chance to just see what happened next. Maybe the best thing he could do for either of them was simply to take each day as it came.

Here. At this place that gave him life and love and hope and didn't deserve to have rocks thrown at it.

He crouched down.

And he placed the rock on the ground.

And he said, finally, decisively, 'I won't.'

Angeline's face twisted. She stomped her foot. She bent her own body down and she picked up the stone and she pulled back her arm, and it was Angeline who broke the window. Which made sense, of course, because it was Angeline who was angry at Direleafe Hall for all it represented – a love and a home that had been denied to her.

It made sense, of course, because Angeline was the one who was meant to perform. Jackdaw was simply meant to watch her.

She peered at Jack, her eyes black diamonds. 'Do you still like me, now, Jack Hollow?' she said.

Jack nodded. 'I do,' he said. 'I do still like you, but ... there should be a limit to all of this, I think. This wildness. Sometimes, it's good to fly, but sometimes it's good, also, to sit and watch the world. It's good to read and learn and be *quiet* for a time. Perhaps one day we could simply sit beside each other on the roof of Direleafe Hall ...'

Angeline leaned close, and she whispered, hot in his ear, 'There are no limits to me, Jack Hollow.'

And then she turned to run but, before she could, a voice cried out, 'Jack Hollow! What is happening here?'

Jack Hollow froze.

Angeline started her running but, at the sound of that same voice again, she too stopped where she was.

The voice said, 'Jack's friend!'

Angeline turned. So, that was something, at least. Angeline turned when a person called her that. When someone called her *Jack's friend*.

So, she still considered herself to be his friend. That was not nothing, either. That was a *lot*.

Mrs Beekman strode out, her voice as close to furious as Jack had ever heard it. She was in her nightgown, a woollen shawl atop it. It was her favourite shawl, Jack knew, made of the fancy kind of wool, dyed the colour of bluebottles, and he knew from his own experience how warm it was.

Sometimes, when winters were particularly cold, they huddled beneath the black blanket *and* the shawl as well. They drank hot cocoa and told stories 'til morning.

That shawl reminded him of love and comfort and softness and all the things – the lack thereof – that had led Angeline to throw that rock.

Mrs Beekman came to Jack's side. 'Are you all right?' she asked him.

That meant everything.

That meant the world.

Because even now – even *now*, when he

had been caught sneaking out, even now when there was a broken window behind him and a rock lying on the floor just beyond it, even *now*, his mother cared the most about Jack and how he felt.

'I'm all right,' he told her, though he wasn't certain at all if it was honestly the truth.

'And that's your friend?' Mrs Beekman asked.

Jack nodded. 'Yes, she is my friend,' he said, and Angeline did not argue.

So that was not nothing, too.

Mrs Beekman nodded and she took a step towards Angeline. 'Jack's friend, did you throw the stone?' she asked.

Angeline was about to confess – Jack saw it all over her face, the varnish turning greyer. She had already, once this day, taken the blame – that time when it was *his* wrongdoing. So, to restore the balance – and even though it pained his heart – Jack Hollow said, 'It was me.'

His mother's face collapsed with disappointment.

And there was nothing worse than the notion that he had disappointed his mother. Disappointing her was worse than anything.

'Will you send me away?' he mumbled.

Mrs Beekman cupped his cheek in her hand and said, 'I will make you clean up this mess.' She gestured at the glass, sparkling prettily like diamonds in the moonlight. 'And then perhaps ...' she leaned closer and whispered, 'for *lying*, I will make you scrub the floors, as I said I might.'

Jackdaw gasped, not for the punishment but for what caused it.

She knew?

She knew he was lying? How could she?

Mrs Beekman nodded – a small, almost imperceptible nod but full of so much knowing – and then she said to Angeline, 'You're shivering.'

Jack looked at his friend and he saw that it was true.

Mrs Beekman – because Mrs Beekman was

good and she was kind and she was loving, and she did not deserve any of this – pulled her bluebottle shawl over her head and she passed it to Angeline. Then, she walked back to her cottage to sleep.

Jack nodded at Angeline. 'I suppose I'd better …' He indicated with his hand, a sort of scrubbing motion. At least, he hoped it looked like that. Angeline just looked at him as if he'd gone peculiar. But, to be fair, she looked at him like this quite often.

As Jack was walking away, towards the kitchen, Angeline called out the most unexpected thing: 'I won't scrub floors,' she said, wrapping the shawl around herself. 'But I will clean up this glass for you.'

He turned. 'You will?'

She nodded. 'I wouldn't for anyone,' she said. 'But I will for you, funny Jackdaw Hollow.' She smiled, just a little. 'You're a bird, you are.'

She crouched and she began to sweep up the glass as she said she would.

And as Jackdaw Hollow left her to go inside and commence his own punishment, he looked up at the windows of Direleafe Hall and he saw the faces of so many girls, staring down at him.

All of them smiled at him.

A couple of them waved.

And none of them seemed to hate him. None of them seemed to fear him or think him strange.

So, that was a thing.

21
The osprey

The three ghost girls tried to warn him about the woman, standing outside, watching as Jack scrubbed the floor.

They had seen her walking along the path towards Direleafe Hall.

They saw, too, Angeline look up and see her monster, approaching. They saw her stand and drop her brush and all the glass fall to the ground again, like magical faerie-formed gemstones, catching the moonlight, reflecting it back, turning the grass to wonderland.

They saw her run, through the gate and away, away, away from her stalking monster.

‘We have to tell him,’ said Florence. ‘She’ll come for him, now the girl is gone.’

But try as they might, they could not catch his eye. They could not make him hear. He seemed to be in a world of his own, deep in thought – about Angeline, they suspected. Or callings.

Or maybe he just didn’t want to hear them.

In the distance, over the hills of the valley that housed Direleafe Hall, far, far away over the apple orchards, a storm began to rumble.

Jack Hollow did not hear it until it was too late.

When he looked out the window, it was not the woman, but Angeline he noticed first. It was always Angeline first. She was already so far away – a distant paleness against the dark sky. Almost as if she were not real. Almost as if he’d imagined her.

And he thought, *I should follow.* But he thought, too, *She wouldn’t like it.*

Perhaps, finally, he was beginning to learn something about Angeline.

The moonlight made her silver. The stars let their dust fall down to rest upon her shoulders upon Mrs Beekman's shawl. And the bluebottle of the shawl and the silver of the stardust combined to make Angeline an angel once more, unearthly and star-made, now and always.

A string was plucked in his heart, a note played that sounded like *goodbye.*

But it wasn't goodbye.

She was only going to Threadneedle House, just over the way where she had always been even before he knew her. So close, even before he knew her.

After this night, he would know her always.

This was not goodbye.

Jack watched until she disappeared completely, and when he closed his eyes she was a cyanotype on his mind. It was only after Angeline had become the stardust, become the night, that Jackdaw saw the other woman.

She stood, ghostlike, at the window.

He made himself be brave and he got to his feet and he walked out to her.

And he knew her. She was the osprey. She was the monster.

'Where is she?' Mrs Bristleroad snarled. 'Where is that girl, Angie Quinn?'

'Quinn,' Jack murmured to himself – so that was the *neveryoumind*.

Mrs Bristleroad stared at him, her bluebell eyes making him shiver. 'Tell me where she is,' she said. 'She must come back to Threadneedle House. She must be punished.'

'No!' Jack cried. 'Why would you punish an orphan ... for *anything*? Haven't we suffered enough?'

Mrs Bristleroad's nose wrinkled. 'Is it *my* fault the girl was born in the mud?' she asked. 'I'll find her, if you won't give her up. I'll find her, and then ...'

'No!' Jack said again. He said it with all his heart and all his soul and all of him – every *piece* of him – and it was like a lightning bolt and like

a thunderclap and Jack felt *powerful*. He roared it, louder: 'No! You will not hurt her! You will not hurt Angeline *ever again*.'

Mrs Bristleroad folded her arms. 'And how,' she said, airily, 'do you mean to stop me?'

'Stomp on her toes,' whispered Nell.

'Stomp *hard*,' said Florence.

'Stomp with all your might,' Lucy added, surprising Jack completely. Lucy had never shown any belligerence before this very moment.

But then, perhaps, he shouldn't have been so shocked. He imagined that people like Mrs Bristleroad could bring out violence in a lamb.

Jack Hollow did not stomp because Jack Hollow was not the violent type. But he had to do something.

And then he remembered. He remembered Mrs Bristleroad's fear on the night he had attempted his haunting. The night he had pretended to be a ghost. Out of the corner of his mouth, he whispered to Lucy, 'You do it. You do the stomping.'

If you've ever had your toes stomped on by a ghost – particularly if you're a person of superstitious bent – you'll understand that it can be quite a disconcerting experience. It was so with this horrible woman.

She let out a little shriek. 'What was that? Who did that?'

Jackdaw looked up at the sky then. He saw six crows, circling, and he remembered another superstition he had learned about in books.

Six crows mean death.

Jack smiled at her. He saw himself in the mirror of her eyes and he saw himself *strong*. He held up his fingers, curled like claws. He opened his mouth and, loud as he could, he let out an ear-shattering, '*Kraa!*'

Angeline had said he was a bird, after all, and the noise felt *right* in his mouth. It felt commanding.

Behind him, he heard a rumbling sound, something like a storm, but not quite.

Bird wings. Beating.

The six crows had stopped their circling and they were flying, flying in a cloud, in a swarm, in a *murder*, towards Mrs Bristleroad.

'Death, Mrs Bristleroad,' Jack called out. 'Six crows mean death, do they not?'

And just then, like magic, a small, black kitten walked across the starlit grass, mewing and purring. It headed straight for Mrs Bristleroad.

Mrs Bristleroad screamed – louder than storms, louder than thunder – and then she turned tail and *ran.*

Jack yelled out after her, 'It's a sign, Mrs Bristleroad. A sign from the universe! When you return to Threadneedle House, not only will you *not* harm Angeline, but you will *leave*. You will resign from your position.'

The crows, as if sensing that this was their moment, *kraaed* as loud as a thunderclap,

and they chased the woman, who looked less like an osprey now and more like a frightened lamb, all the way back to Threadneedle House.

Jack's every limb unstiffened. Joy flooded into his lungs, filled every inch of him.

Angeline was safe.

He turned and was surprised to see Mrs Beekman with tears in her eyes, holding the small, black kitten.

'You saw that?' he whispered.

She nodded. 'It was magic. What you did there. That was magic.'

Jack took her hands.

'I'm so very sorry,' he said. 'About the sneaking and the lying and the window and everything.'

Mrs Beekman shook her head. 'No, no, my Jack,' she whispered. 'I ... have failed you.'

Jack shook his head, furiously. 'That's nonsense,' he said. 'You've loved me, always. You gave me a home, when I had none. You gave me a *family*.'

'You gave me mine,' said Mrs Beekman.

Jack blushed. 'I heard you. You said you might send me away ...'

Mrs Beekman shook her head, furiously. 'Nonsense talk,' she whispered. 'Just the anxious murmurings of a mother who loves her son to the ends of the earth.' She smiled.

Jack Hollow, relief flooding his heart, still could not quite believe it. 'I am not great, like my parents were. Their callings were big and kind and *worthy* and the whole community loved them. I think I might know my calling, now, but it is small and simple and not special. I am not special.'

'Oh, Jack Hollow!' Mrs Beekman cried. 'Here is the truth of it – you are special simply for being *you.* Your greatness was achieved the moment you came into my arms. You charmed me. You transformed *everything,* in that very moment. You do not need to give me anything else.'

She wiped at Jack's tears with the coarse

pad of her thumb. 'Shall we go inside and have some hot cocoa and we can tell each other stories until the sunrise? The only trouble of it all will be that I have given away my shawl and I can't find my blanket.'

Jack's cheeks burned. 'Never mind,' he mumbled. 'Telling stories with you, even without any blankets, would make me very happy indeed. The cocoa will warm us. And I love sunrises, almost as much as midnights. And then, in the morning, can I go and see Angeline?'

Mrs Beekman's eyes narrowed. 'You know you would miss double mathematics.'

Jack nodded.

Mrs Beekman smiled and, for a moment, she looked so many years younger. For a moment, she looked like a child. 'Well,' she said. 'Just so.'

They sat inside together, huddled, warming as – outside – the rain began to fall.

22
Mr Hardbread

The following morning, Jack stood at the door of Threadneedle House.

The man who answered Jack's knocking had a face like the side of a mountain, his mouth a downturned cave carved at its base. He had two furry eyebrows, like charred hedges, and his nose was a rocky protrusion. His eyes were unmistakeably kind.

When Jack Hollow knocked on the door, it took the man a full minute to open it, and he did so with an impatient, 'What is it, now?'

Jack, startled, could not think what to answer.

'I'll warn ye,' the man said, poking a cracked, dirty finger. The finger shook some, as if this forcefulness was an effort. 'I've had a morning of it already, so if ye're here to sell *en-cy-clo-paedias*, I've no need for learning, in my profession. If ye're here to give me the word of our Lord, I already know it. If ye're here to report a lost bird, I've found her again – for the hundredth time, I'd wager. So, I'll ask once more, what *is* it, boy?'

Jack finally located his words – bolstered by the knowledge that his purpose here at Threadneedle House did not fall into any of the man's proscribed categories. 'I'm not here because of a bird,' he said (although, of course, the truth of it was that Jack Hollow was only here at *all* because of a bird). 'I'm here to collect Angeline.'

The hedge eyebrows bunched. 'Come again? Who're ye referring to?'

'Angeline,' Jack said, more clearly. 'She works here, at Threadneedle House.'

The man took a moment, stitching Jack's words together in his mind. His eyes widened. 'Aha,' he said. 'Ye're speaking of Miss Angie Quinn.'

'Angie. Yes,' said Jack, remembering that Mrs Bristleroad had also called her this. He wondered who had made the decision to prune the flowers off Angeline's name – whether she had done it on her own, as a way to distance herself from this place, or whether the people of Threadneedle House had done it to her, to diminish her. He was so busy mulling this question that he missed the man's reply. 'I'm sorry,' he said. 'Could you repeat that?'

'I *said*,' the man repeated, more loudly, 'that Miss Quinn is no longer a member of the household staff of Threadneedle House. She left our company in the wee hours of this very morning, along with – but not *accompanying*, if you take my meaning – Mrs Winifred Bristleroad, housekeeper. Suffice to say, all of these departures form much of the reason why my day has been *a day*, already.' The man scowled, even harder. 'So, if ye don't mind—'

Jack could hear a storm wind inside his head, could hear a hurricane.

Angeline had *departed*?

Angeline had *gone*?

No.

He looked up at the sky, as if the stars might come out in the daytime, as if they all might rain down upon him and turn him into dust.

The man made to close the door. 'Wait!' Jack cried, holding out his hand.

The man raised one eyebrow, his nostrils flaring.

'Where ... where has she gone?' Jack asked, in a small voice. 'Do you know?'

'I know where she *says* she was off to,' the man replied.

'Where did she say she was ... off to?' Jack asked.

The man folded his arms. 'En-light-en me, why I should be telling ye?'

'Because she is my friend,' Jack said, simply. 'I am the only boy at Direleafe Hall. I have no friends there, which is perhaps my failing and one I plan to rectify. I see ghosts, three of them. I am pointy of nose and feathery of hair and small and shy and have nothing much to recommend me. But I had Angeline, for a little while. I cared for her and I believe, somewhere beneath her varnish, she cared for me. I need to know where she is and that she's safe. Mrs Beekman has kept me safe, my whole life, after the lightning bolt that killed my parents and should have killed me, but nobody has ever done that for Angeline. I want to be her safety. I want to ...' Jackdaw trailed off.

The man was staring at him. 'Lightning bolt ...' he whispered. 'Jackdaw Hollow. Well, I'll be.'

Jack couldn't be sure, but it seemed as though the sturdy old man was blinking back tears.

He nodded, curtly. 'All right,' he said. He

reached into the pocket of his moth-holed tweed coat and pulled out a folded sheet of paper. 'Found this in her room,' he said. 'She came back to pack her things, I expect, and she left this. I expect it is for you, ain't it?'

He passed the letter across and cleared his throat. 'Jackdaw Hollow.' He nodded. 'Just so. Just so. Knew your parents,' he added, gruffly. 'Fine people. Dreadful shame. My boy, Arthur, runs the old orchard now, did ye know? So, if ye ever were of a mind to go there ...'

Jack was surprised to feel tears in his eyes. 'Thank you,' he said.

'They were so proud of ye, son,' the man said, gently. 'Ye were the apple of their eye. Ye made a difference in their lives, if only fer a short time. And I'll place bets you made a difference to Angie. All over the Midlands people talk of how love for you transformed that Mrs Beekman. Made her want to live again. You gave her love. That should carry a boy through, shouldn't it?'

Mr Hardbread took a deep breath and wobbled slightly on his feet, as if the effort of making such a long and heartfelt speech had knocked the wind right out of him.

'Thank you,' Jack said, wiping at his eye. 'Mr ...'

'Hardbread. Walter Hardbread. I expect your Angeline told you I'm a right grump.'

Jack nodded, sheepishly. 'But she said you're kind as well.'

'I never used to be a grump,' Mr Hardbread sighed. 'Sometimes, life does things to you, d'ye understand? But it don't mean it ain't worth living.'

Jack nodded. He did understand.

Jack looked down at the folded paper. He saw, written on it in Angeline's shaky hand, the words *My Friend*.

'Thank you,' he told the old mountain of a man.

The man nodded. 'Just so,' he said, again.

'I think ...' Jack said, slowly. 'I think you're

not a grump at all, really. I think you are very kind, inside.'

Mr Hardbread nodded and cleared his throat several times. 'Well, now,' he said, finally. He looked into the distance for a little while, before looking back at Jackdaw. 'Ye're a clever boy, aren't you?' he said.

Jack smiled. 'I suppose I am.'

'How would you feel ...' Mr Hardbread said, softly, and with cheeks as pink as galah feathers, 'about teaching an old man to read?'

★

When Jack arrived back at Direleafe Hall, he didn't go straight to Mrs Beekman's cottage. Instead, he searched for the perfect place to read Angeline's letter. Eventually, he settled on a silver birch tree, beside the front wall. He had never noticed this tree before. His head was usually in books and, lately, in a tulip field. But now, the tree seemed to call to him. It shimmered ghostily, like the girls.

Jackdaw Hollow sat for a very long time,

alone, and he let himself be sad. He let himself be as sad as his body needed. Angeline was gone. What would become of him, now?

He let every tear that wished it, fall. He let every sad feeling be as big as it needed.

The three ghost girls watched, at a respectful distance, quiet and sad, too, in their hearts. They had not expected it to turn out this way.

But that was life, wasn't it? Nothing but a big *unexpected.*

When the sun began to fade, when Jack's shoulders had stilled, when his tears had abated, only then did they climb the tree with him. They perched on branches, and Nell said, 'I'm sorry.'

Jack, startled – both at their appearance and Nell's unusual meekness – blurted, 'It's all right.'

'It's not. I said that she would be a good friend to you and that she would teach you to find your calling. A good friend doesn't leave you, so she wasn't that. And she taught you nothing at all.'

Jack shook his head. 'Really, Nell. It's all right. It did me good, to feel all that. It did me good, to be wild, and it did me good to learn that human beings are not characters and life is not a story. Angeline did teach me, I think. She did not show me what my calling should be, but she showed me how to open my heart enough to look for it. And ... it did me good, I think, to cry.'

Nell pouted. 'So, I apologised for nothing?'

Jack let himself smile. 'Not nothing, Nell. I think that part did you good, too.'

Nell crossed her arms. 'What about your calling?'

Jack sighed. He looked out at the wide, blue sky. He saw the crows, still circling. He wondered what they searched for. 'I have an idea,' he said. 'Or perhaps I have no idea. And perhaps that's just fine.'

Jack felt a tingling on his fingers. He looked down. Nell was holding his hand.

'I'm sorry,' she said, again.

‘I see that,’ he replied. More quietly, he said, ‘I see you.’

Nell cleared her throat, loudly. ‘Well, ain’t you going to read her letter, then?’

Jack nodded. He smiled. ‘Will you read it with me? I think I need my best friends around me while I read it.’

All three girls grew an inch with pride when he said that, though Nell tried her best to hide it.

Jack opened the letter, slowly, and they peeped over his shoulder as he read.

23
The letter

My friend (all right, you may call yourself that now) Jackdaw Hollow,

I know you have taught me all the big, good words. I wish I could use them all now. But I ain't got time, I'm afeared! I certainly do not have time to try to spell them in a way that would not make you shake your head and sigh. I hardly have the time to write this letter at all!

I am about to run, Jack. Finally, I am about to run. Mayperhaps this will make you sad – I hope not too sad, though. You have enough sadness inside you. You need more happiness. And I do, too, Jack Hollow. I am hoping I will find it, where I am running to.

I am running away to the circus.

I do not want you to think you did not give me happiness. I had such a lark with you, being wild. It was nice, to have a friend. But I was never meant to stay here, in this place. I am ever meant for the circus.

I do know you wanted to save me. I'm sorry I couldn't let you. See, I've been saving myself for a long time and it's part of my pride. And my armour. Mayperhaps one day I'll let someone help. But not now. Not 'til I'm properly where I should be. I need my armour, to get there.

You were a good teacher, though. The best.

One day, I might have a bairn of my own and I might send her to Direleafe Hall to meet you. Mayperhaps you might teach her like you taught me. I will tell her to tell you stories of her mother and how she flew on the flying trapeze. How she flew all the way to the stars.

I have a question for you: do you think your Mrs Beekman would mind very much if I took her knitted shawl with me? It is quite cosy and makes me think of some kind of ghostly feeling I have of what a home might be.

I hope one day you will fly as well.

All my love, and all the tulips and all the thistles, too. I'm glad you didn't throw that rock.

Goodbye, Jack Hollow.

Angeline Quinn

24
Just as he should be

When he had finished reading the letter, Jack folded it neatly, placed it in his pocket and he leaned back on the trunk of the silver birch tree and looked up at the stars.

Some part of him – he couldn't decide if it was a big part or a small one – felt so happy for Angeline.

But some of him was sad, as well, for himself.

He didn't say anything to the ghost girls, but he knew they were there. He knew they would always be there. And that was a comfort.

The ghost girls didn't say anything to Jack Hollow, either. This was not a time for talking, they knew. This was a time for breaking and healing and breathing in and letting go.

But they held Jack Hollow tight in their arms.

They would hold him tightly, for always. And Mrs Beekman would hold him tightly, too, for as many years as God gave her. They all hoped that would be enough.

And down below them all, a girl with disobedient curls held a basket of apples, a pat of butter and a sack of flour, and she sat with a small, black kitten and waited for Jackdaw to come and try again at making pies.

She hoped that would be enough.

And above them all, the stars began to twinkle. They shone down on Jackdaw Hollow and they were very happy with the boy who sat in their light.

He was just as he should be.

He always had been.

Epilogue

Jackdaw Hollow lived his whole life at Direleafe Hall. He was brought there, pink and whimpering, and he died there, bent and silver-haired.

But before that, Jackdaw Hollow *lived.*

And it was not only those moments – in the tulip field, with the girl who was not an angel – that made up his life. Those moments were golden, but life is a series of moments, golden and grey, and every one of them is a treasure.

Life is a treasure and a perfect, impossible miracle, and this was true for Jackdaw Hollow more than for most.

It was his calling. Having survived, *living* was his calling.

Jack's life was what came before Angeline. It was what came after. It was *especially* what came after.

He befriended some of the Direleafe girls who had waved at him from their windows. He tutored some of them and helped them to find their own callings. They became lifelong friends.

He befriended Mr Hardbread, too. He taught him to read, and Mr Hardbread taught him much more in return. He never told Jack it was he who found him, that stormy night, when he was a babe. He didn't want the boy to believe that he owed him anything.

Jack made extra special friends, too, with Angharad. They married, but both understood that it was a marriage of friendship, not love – at least, not of the romantic kind – but the love between friends is almost more special, isn't it?

They had a small, black cat, called Solace. She was their pride and joy.

He never did improve at his pie-making. But that didn't matter. It was the trying that counted.

Jack shared his life with Angharad.

But most of all, he shared his life with his mother, Mrs Beekman. She taught him all she knew about being a teacher. He taught her some things in return.

At night, they stayed up late, learning together and at the end of it, even as he grew older, she sang him a song – a song she had first heard in her dreams.

My small, precious hatchling,
In your nest, tucked in tight,
Flutter down your eyelids
And bid the stars goodnight ...

On Mrs Beekman's last day in this world, he sang the song to her. When he had finished, she sighed, so quietly he almost missed it.

'You were the greatest gift of my life, Jack Hollow.' She gripped his arms. 'You,' she said, more loudly, 'made all the difference in the world to me. And that is enough. That is *more* than enough. To make a difference in the life of even one person ... that is a life's good work, Jack Hollow. You were my life. You were my whole universe.'

Jack cleared his throat, willing those insubordinate tears away. They would not comply. They came, anyway. 'I don't know what to say.'

His mother nodded. 'Just say you'll be all right. That's all I need to hear. That's all a mother needs to hear.'

'I'll be all right,' he promised her.

Mrs Beekman nodded. 'Just so,' she whispered.

'You were the greatest gift of my life,' he whispered back to her. 'You made all the difference in the world to me. I promise I will take care of Direleafe Hall, for you. I hope I do it in a way that makes you proud.'

And so, Jack Hollow became the headmaster of Direleafe Hall. Perhaps teaching had always been his calling. Maybe it was some of it. But birds and stars and cocoa were, too.

They loved him, all the Direleafe girls, for his heart and his imagination. He told them every precious thing that he had ever learned and ever known. He told them all about his origins. He kept nothing secret, nothing a mystery, and so, there was nothing to fear about their most peculiar headmaster.

He ran with them and read with them and made each of them feel at *home.* They were their own miraculous people. Each of them strange in their own ways. Each of them so special and destined for great things.

He helped them find their callings.

He climbed the silver birch tree, for as long as he was able, and sometimes climbed onto the roof as well. He liked sitting up there on the first day of every year to watch the new girls arrive.

Birds came to sit beside him. They trusted him, now. They knew he would never try to cage them. The ghosts sat with him, too. They were his very most cherished companions, always.

Jackdaw Hollow had so much to be joyful for in his wild and wonderful life. And he was, mostly, as happy as his friends the birds.

It was only sometimes, when Jackdaw Hollow sat on the roof of Direleafe Hall, watching the stars, that sadness crept into his soul. Sadness is in all of us, after all, no matter how hard we try to escape it, and it is even more inescapable when we have a beginning to life like the one Jackdaw Hollow had.

He was sad for his birth parents and for all he had lost when that lightning bolt fell from the sky.

He was sad, too, for the loss of Angeline, and of Mr Hardbread, and of his mother Mrs Beekman.

But the sadness was not all of him. It was only a sapling within him. Inside Jackdaw Hollow, there was an entire forest.

Jackdaw Hollow never took Mr Hardbread up on his offer to see the orchard while the old man lived. Jack feared his heart could not take it – seeing the place where his parents died and where his life changed irrevocably.

It was only when he knew he was dying, at the age of seventy-six – when a doctor had told him that the forest within him was losing its leaves and the last days of winter were coming – that Jack made himself be brave. He had led such a happy, joyful life, after all, but it felt as though there was one part of it missing.

The orchard was that part.

On the very last day of Jack Hollow's life, he kissed his best friend, and wife, Angharad, goodbye, and she tried not to feel too sad. She gave him a pie to take with him.

Angharad and the three ghost girls watched him go, and the three ghost girls held each other, and they held Angharad, too. She could not see them but, somehow, she felt them.

When he had disappeared from sight,

Angharad turned and looked back up at Direleafe Hall, and she thought, *Well, I suppose this is mine now.* And she became the headmistress of Direleafe.

She adopted an orphaned girl who came to live at the hall and, in time, that daughter became headmistress, too. And so, the hall continued to live and breathe and grow.

But that was all the future. For now, Angharad and the ghosts stood at the gates of Direleafe Hall.

'I suppose he'll remain in the orchard,' Nell said, 'if that is where he dies.'

'Maybe he'll return to us, somehow,' said Florence, hopefully.

'Maybe he'll fly,' Lucy whispered.

★

Jackdaw Hollow sat beneath an apple tree that had signs of scarring on its bark that might have been from a lightning bolt. He did not know for sure that it was the right tree, but it felt like it might be.

A crow sat on a branch above him. The crow let out a single *kraa* and Jack looked up at it, *right at it* ... and he felt something inside of him shift. Some piece fell into place.

And then, Jack Hollow smiled and closed his eyes.

★

When he opened his eyes – a moment later, or it might have been twenty years – he could *see* all the colours.

When he opened his eyes, he could *hear* so many other noises: the whisperings of the trees, the whisperings of the stars.

When he opened his eyes, he was Hollowbeak Crow and he was sitting in the silver birch tree at Direleafe Hall.

He did not remember his life before, except that he had been a boy and he had been loved and he had lived.

And living was his calling.

Down below him, students tumbled through the high iron gates that separated the school from all of the world. The gates were as old and life-worn as the hall itself, but the children were new and clean and shining.

They moved in through the arched wooden doors, the hinges browned and groaning with age. And then they were swallowed up by the door, by the grey brick walls, by the stones. They were a school of blue-and-grey-scaled fish, made shining by the sea, swimming into the mouth of a whale.

All except for two of them.

That last two.

Only, one of them was not a student at all. She was a woman. She carried a leather bag and wore the determined face of a teacher on her first day.

Beside her, there was a little girl with dark hair and eyes, and skin so pale that, when the sunlight bounced off it, she seemed to glow.

Like an angel.

They were greeted at the gates by a severe-looking woman. Hollowbeak turned so he

could make out what they were saying. He heard only two words:

Wonder and *Quinn.*

He watched as the girl, clasping her mother's hand, followed the severe-looking woman in through the door of Direleafe Hall.

Right before the hall swallowed them up, the girl looked towards the silver birch tree.

She caught Hollowbeak's eye.

And she smiled.

So, that was a thing.

And somehow, all the pieces clicked into place, then. The scale of his life reached a perfect balance. He was here, now, in this form and on this day, because of her.

Hollowbeak whispered to himself, *Wonder.*

And then he whispered, *Just so.*

Acknowledgements

This book, like every book, is for my daughter. I write everything for her. I am grateful, every day, for her inspiration. She lights up the world.

I am enormously grateful to so many people who made this book come to life. My agent, Brian, always in my corner, believing in the strange, dark little worlds I create and fighting to show them to the world.

Clair, always, for her kindness, compassion, humanity ... and her amazing talent as an editor and publisher. Clair, you are the duck's guts.

Cathy, for being there with me every step of the way, gently guiding me in the right direction with her wisdom and just generally being an exceptional human being.

Kristy, who completely shaped this book into what it is, showing me with such grace all the places where it could be strengthened. Kristy, I have loved working on these books with you. You are just exemplary.

Rachel, who made the characters literally come to life in ways I could never have imagined possible.

Jean, for pushing me out of my comfort zone and showing me I can do things I didn't think I could do.

Kate and Denise and everyone at UQP, thank you for making me feel like family.

I want to thank my own, real life family, close and extended, for always, always supporting me in this strange endeavour. It's not a normal life, being a writer, or being the loved one of a writer. You're all such wonderful humans, to have stood by me all this time. I love you all.

'Joey's Apple', you know who you are. I couldn't do this without your humour, solidarity and memes.

I want to thank my cat for curling up beside me while I write, Josh Ritter for providing the soundtrack, and gluten-free biscuit makers of all persuasions for providing the snacks.

I want to thank all the kids who have read these books and got in touch – all the brilliant, brave, clever, funny, imaginative readers who make all of this worthwhile.

All of you, you are lights in the world. Thank you for shining.

Kate Gordon grew up in a small town by the sea in Tasmania. She is the author of six novels for teenagers, as well as the picture books *Bird on a Wire* and *Amira's Magpie*, and the junior fiction series *Juno Jones*. Her middle-grade books include *The Heartsong of Wonder Quinn*, *The Ballad of Melodie Rose*, and *Aster's Good, Right Things*, which was shortlisted in the Speech Pathology Book of the Year Awards and won the 2021 CBCA Book of the Year for Younger Readers.

Kate's books have been published internationally. *Girl Running, Boy Falling* and *Aster's Good, Right Things* have both been adapted for the stage.

When not writing, Kate reads, listens to Josh Ritter, has grand adventures with her daughter, and is (finally) learning to drive a car.

First published 2022 by University of Queensland Press
PO Box 6042, St Lucia, Queensland 4067 Australia

University of Queensland Press (UQP) acknowledges the Traditional Owners and their custodianship of the lands on which UQP operates. We pay our respects to their Ancestors and their descendants, who continue cultural and spiritual connections to Country. We recognise their valuable contributions to Australian and global society.

uqp.com.au
reception@uqp.com.au

Cover design and illustration by Rachel Tribout
Internal illustrations by Rachel Tribout
Author photograph by Stephen Lovell
Typeset in 13/20 pt Adobe Text Pro by Post Pre-press Group, Brisbane
Printed in Australia by McPherson's Printing Group

Australian Government | Australia Council for the Arts

University of Queensland Press is assisted by the Australian Government through the Australia Council, its arts funding and advisory body.

A catalogue record for this book is available from the National Library of Australia.

ISBN 978 0 7022 6348 4 (pbk)
ISBN 978 0 7022 6643 0 (epdf)
ISBN 978 0 7022 6644 7 (epub)
ISBN 978 0 7022 6645 4 (kindle)

University of Queensland Press uses papers that are natural, renewable and recyclable products made from wood grown in well-managed forests and other controlled sources. The logging and manufacturing processes conform to the environmental regulations of the country of origin.

FSC www.fsc.org
MIX
Paper from responsible sources
FSC® C001695